Born to Race

By BLANCHE CHENERY PERRIN

Illustrated by Sam Savitt

SCHOLASTIC BOOK SERVICES
NEW YORK · TORONTO · LONDON · AUCKLAND · SYDNEY · TOKYO

7th printing . . . . February 1972

Printed in the U.S.A.

Chapter ONE

THE FARM WAS IN VIRGINIA and was still called Cherry-dale, though there were only a few cherry trees left from the old orchards. Now, horses were raised there.

Suzy Taylor, whose father owned the farm, thought horses were the loveliest, most exciting crop any farmer could wish for. Cherries were delicious, but not to be mentioned in the same breath with the twenty or so prancy little foals which arrived every spring.

These horses were all Thoroughbreds, and the best of them were trained to race — trained here on the farm. Half a dozen foals had already been born this spring, and now Suzy was waiting impatiently for Falada's foal to appear. Falada was Suzy's favorite of the hundred horses on the farm, and Suzy herself had named her after the horse in *The Prince and the Goose Girl*.

Not much more than a year ago, Falada had been racing. Everyone thought then she was the prettiest thing on the farm, and the fastest. In what turned out to be

1

her final race, Falada had led for more than half a mile; the real contest had been between her and a chestnut, Dark Son. Falada kept her lead, though Dark Son had whittled it down to half a length when his jockey began using the whip. As the whip came stinging down on his flank, Dark Son sprang slightly to one side. This crowded Falada who bumped into the rail fencing the track.

She stumbled, bounced against the rail again, and

this time fell. Her jockey fell, too — but Mac rolled over under the fence in a compact ball out of the way of the thudding hoofs of the other horses. The pack tore by. Mac slowly picked himself up and stood dizzily. Falada struggled to her feet, too. She started to hobble home, no longer part of the galloping field, her proud head hanging. She whimpered with pain.

Mac recovered quickly — he had only had the breath knocked out of him. But Falada's injuries were more serious. She had plainly torn a ligament, but it took X-ray pictures to show the long crack that ran down the big bone of her right foreleg.

The vet shook his head: Falada would recover, but it was unlikely that she would race again. Now the problem was how to get her back to Cherrydale, the Virginia farm where she had been bred and trained, and where she might recover.

When her father finished his story, Suzy burst into tears. She tried to hide them — at eleven you are not supposed to cry — and turned her face away so that only her red curls showed.

"Oh, Daddy, what are you going to *do*?" she asked, her face still hidden. Suzy had lived all her life at Cherrydale and understood that a horse with a broken leg usually must be destroyed. The leg cannot heal if the horse stands on it, and, she well knew, no horse can be kept lying down for the several weeks needed for real recovery.

"Stop crying, Sue. The bone is cracked, not broken.

3

But with the torn ligaments and so on, it's likely to heal stiff."

"Then what — ?"

"We can't decide now. We'll have to wait and see. But it's serious, Sue, and not just because we love Falada. I was counting on the money she'd win to help pay for the new stable — and your camp this summer, for that matter."

"The new stable — my camp — ?" Suzy echoed.

"The new stable, your camp," her father repeated, and looked at his daughter curiously. "How did you think I paid for things, anyway?"

"I guess I never thought."

"I guess you never did. We'll talk about it later." And he started off for his office in the far corner of the broodmare barn.

Suzy started to follow him, but the office was forbidden territory, so she looked for Ben, the head stableman and a friend of hers. Ben was tall, with cheeks the color of warm gingerbread, and Suzy thought he knew almost as much about horses as if he were one himself. Now she asked, "Ben, have you any idea when Falada can come home?"

"Soon as she's able to travel. The vet and the trainer, they're working out some kind of fancy sling arrangement for the van, so's to keep the weight off her leg. Soon's they've got that fixed, we'll be seeing Miss Falada again."

Six weeks had gone by before the veterinarian would allow Falada to be driven the four hundred miles home from the race track in New York. The time seemed long to Suzy. Every afternoon as she came home from school she looked hopefully to see if the horse van bringing Falada had arrived. In the meantime, she tried to make some plans. She had had a long conversation with her father and thought she now understood how things were. "I want to talk about money," she had said to him. The deep lines that usually meant he was worried appeared in his forehead.

"You need money?" he asked.

"No, sir — but — well, where do we get it?"

"We get it, when we have it, from the horses. This is a stock farm, Sue. You know that. Now listen to some a-b-c. We breed horses, we raise horses, we train horses, we put them in races to prove how good they are. Every race has a purse, or prize. The purse might be as low as a thousand dollars. But the big races have big purses up to one hundred thousand dollars or more. We thought Falada was good enough to run in the big races."

"She was!" Suzy interrupted.

"We expected the purses she'd win would help pay for all the food the horses eat, the food we eat, too, pay the stable boys, pay the trainer, and pay for the new stable. Even for your camp. Now do you understand?"

"Don't the other horses win anything? How about Julia's Pride?"

"Of course they do, but Falada was our best. It's like

5

the wage earner in a family being ill or laid off."

"Daddy, how could you build the new stable before the horses had won the money for it?"

Mr. Taylor laughed. "I had some. And I borrowed the rest from the bank on a note. That's a promise to pay later."

A loan! Suzy shivered. Suppose Daddy *couldn't* pay it back? Would the bank come and sell the horses and the farm, take away everything she loved?

She walked to the window and stared out at the big paddock. Most of the things dear to her seemed to be there, the rolling fields, the narrow brown river edging them, the group of yearlings grazing peacefully. Then one of them — was it Danny Boy? — gave a snort and started running. The others pursued him in what seemed a game of follow-the-leader. She couldn't bear to lose any of this, she loved it all too much.

She turned back to her father. "Daddy, what will you *do?*"

"We'll manage. When and if Falada is well, I've made up my mind to breed her. Maybe she'll have a foal who'll turn out to be as good as she is."

A foal! Suzy loved all the foals; every year, when the new ones appeared, it seemed the same lovely miracle. But Falada's foal would be special, different, better than all the rest. She asked, keeping her voice matter of fact, "Who'll you breed her to?"

"Big Claus, I think. And if the foal should have his stamina and Falada's speed, we'll sweep everything else off the tracks. In the meantime — and it is a mean time because it'll be long — we'll have to economize everywhere we can. We'll all work and save, but I'm afraid camp is out for you this year."

Suzy struggled with her throat. It felt large and dry. It stung so she could not speak. Not to go to camp? Daddy couldn't mean it. Summer *was* camp. She loved the cool Maine woods and Pine Lake just outside her cabin door, shimmering up at her in the early summer sunlight. "Don't think about it," she told herself. "Put your mind on remembering you're probably going to keep the farm and the horses."

Two or three days went by, and Suzy wondered desperately what she could do to help — with the farm, and just perhaps, get herself to camp. After much thought, she knocked timidly at the office door.

Her father's brows shot up when he saw his caller, and Suzy said hastily, "I came to the office because it's on business. Ben said Falada's sure to come home next week. I want to take care of her, bring her feed, groom her, everything. I — I thought," she added, "it would save money for me to do the work. And you know how I love Falada."

Mr. Taylor's brows had returned to their normal position, and he looked at his daughter seriously. "That's a very handsome offer, my dear. But I don't want to overwork you while school is going on. Talk to your mother, and if she thinks it's all right, I'll accept. I've been doing some figuring, and had just made up my mind to let one of the stable boys go. It would be a real help if you could take up some of the slack. But see what your mother says first."

She got up, feeling older and rather solemn, and her father got up, too, and escorted her to the office door. She started to shake hands but her father bent and kissed her. "I think this is still all right," he said, "even granting you may be a stable boy."

Her mother was more of a problem and at first said a decided "No!" Suzy started to beg, but then changed her mind and said in a reasonable tone, "Daddy doesn't think the work would be too hard for me. He said I'd be a real help."

"I'm sure you would, honey. And I suppose you have enough time. But if you're around Ben all the time, you'll be talking and acting just like him — chewing tobacco, too, probably." She laughed. "I want to keep my *girl*."

"Ben chews only because Daddy doesn't allow smoking around the stables. I promise I won't do anything you don't like."

"Well — " Mrs. Taylor hesitated. But it was a permission, and by the time Falada was due back Suzy was ready to take over her care.

When the big blue van pulled into the stable yard, Suzy, who had been sitting on the top rail of the fence watching for its arrival, jumped down. The van came to rest with its doors opposite the mounting block, and Suzy stepped in as soon as they were opened. Falada

8

stood in one of the box stalls, broad bands of canvas running under her belly to make a sort of cradle to take the weight off her injured leg.

"Leave her be!" Ben called as Suzy started toward Falada's head. "She's tired and nervous. Let her get settled down before you touch her."

Suzy spread her legs in a defiant stance. "*I'm* supposed to look after Falada. *I'm* her stable boy."

"Stable boys mind the stable boss — that's *me*," said Ben. He entered the van and, after some prolonged coaxing, reappeared leading Falada. She stepped gingerly from the van to the ramp — and — "Now, Suzy," Ben called.

In a moment, Suzy was at Falada's other side, patting her shoulder and murmuring consolingly. The big mare limped slowly down the ramp.

Once on home soil Falada seemed to improve rapidly. Suzy spent a good deal of her time in the stall with Falada, in addition to doing the necessary feeding, watering, and throwing in of clean straw.

"Falada's awful sick of this stall," she complained to Ben. "Can't we let her out? She's lonesome for the other horses."

"She'll just have to take you for company," said Ben. "She might get hurt worse. You know how they all get to fooling. You take any chances with Falada and I'll get me a new stable boy."

"Ben! You wouldn't!"

"Not if you're a good nurse, I won't."

9

It was just after this conversation that Suzy had a chance to prove how good a nurse she was. Falada — turning suddenly in her stall — bumped her injured leg. A few hours later it had begun to swell, and the flesh could be seen puffing over the top of the bandage.

"We got to tell your papa, but I don't think we need Dr. Plumm yet," Ben said, feeling the leg carefully. Falada laid her ears back — even his gentle touch hurt — and he released her at once. "She's got a little fever in that leg. You and me can get rid of it. Let's try a wet dressing."

He gave Suzy directions as to just what to do. "And you be careful," he concluded. "When Falada's leg hurts, she don't remember whether or not you're a friend."

Suzy nodded. She had been frightened more than once when a horse had suddenly reared and seemed trying to box with flailing front hoofs.

For the next four days Suzy spent almost every minute she was not at school working on Falada. Water was piped to the stables, but Ben thought it ought to be warm for the treatments, so Suzy lugged buckets from the kitchen to Falada's stall. This was hard work. Suzy was tired and looked it. When Ben tried to relieve her, she was indignant. "You do all the night work. I'm keeping the day."

The next night she was so tired she dropped off to sleep over her homework. Her mother wakened her. "I won't have you working so hard. You're worn out. To-morrow — "

"Please let me do my job," said Suzy. "It'll just be a day or two more. We think the swelling's starting to go down. Please, Mummie!"

"Just one more day, then," said her mother reluctantly.

Luckily, when a heavy-eyed Suzy went out next morning to give Falada a before-school treatment, the leg was down to normal size. Dr. Plumm came by that afternoon on one of his routine visits, and Suzy stood nearby anxiously as he removed the bandage and took a long look at the injured leg.

"It's coming along fine," he said. "Nature's been good to Falada and she's had good care. I guess that means you, Ben."

"It means Suzy," Ben said.

Suzy stared. Ben wasn't much given to praise, and the joy she felt at hearing his words spread into a wide smile as she looked at him.

Not long after this, Falada was bred to Big Claus, himself a famous racer once. Suzy had thought she could not wait the long months for the foal's arrival, especially after Dad had said again there could be no camp for her that year. Until that minute she hadn't realized how much she had hoped that somehow the money for camp could be squeezed out. But she knew from her father's expression that his decision was final.

"I hate to disappoint you when you've worked like a real staver," he said. "Ben says he'd hire you any day.

But we can't spend money I haven't got. Next year perhaps —"

"How about the bank loan?" Suzy almost forgot her disappointment about camp in her fears for the farm.

"Well, we've made economies — you've shared them, Sue — and we've paid off a bit. The bank isn't pressing

13

us more than it should." He ran his fingers worriedly through his hair. "We've got some good horses coming along, and if Falada will just kindly produce the top-notcher we expect — "

"If she does — ?"

"We'd beat everything running on the tracks, and your doting father would send you on a trip to the moon, instead of camp!" He and Suzy both laughed.

This was all in the past. Falada had been bred, and the time was now near when her foal should arrive.

It was barely six o'clock on an April morning when her mother came into Suzy's room hurriedly. "Wake up!" She shook Suzy. "Dad says run to the stable — "

Suzy tore into her clothes and raced the short distance from the house. Her father and Ben were already in the stable. On the straw of Falada's stall lay what looked like a long, roly-poly sausage, but turned out to be the new foal. Its legs were snugly folded against its body, its head, with little perky ears, resting on the forehoofs. It lay on the straw a few minutes, looking around with misty eyes, and then gave a long, low whicker. After that, it rose to its feet. The watching men sighed with relief: a foal that is slow to get up is likely to be weak. The new baby's long slim legs looked very unsteady, but she did not seem to notice, and glanced around inquiringly.

"A filly!" breathed Mr. Taylor, and if there was disappointment in his tone, Suzy did not notice it.

14

"Another girl on the farm — that'll be fun!" she said. "Dad, may I touch her just once, just to pet her?" Her eager hands were already stretched out.

"Not yet. Just watch Falada. She'll lick every inch of that baby before she's through."

Falada struggled to her feet and was now busy licking her foal. Suzy gave her father a questioning glance. "I should think that big, rough tongue running all over the baby would hurt."

"Every new baby gets a bath. You did. Besides, this is a mare's way of learning to know her foal. When Falada finishes, she'll have the baby's own special smell so thoroughly, she'll be able to find her even in the dark."

Meanwhile Falada had continued to lick the little filly until she was thoroughly washed. Then Ben stepped forward and dried the baby off with a rough towel. She got a vigorous rub and did not like it much, because, like most babies, she was hungry. As soon as Ben released her, she snuggled up to her mother and looked for food.

A cow's milk bag hangs low and is easily seen, but a mare's is high and has to be searched for. The little foal fumbled around, smelling her mother's chest and legs, and Suzy, watching, hopped from one foot to the other in impatience.

"She's hungry! Daddy, why don't you show her where her food is?"

"She'll find it," said Mr. Taylor placidly.

"How'll she know when she's in the right place?"

Mr. Taylor laughed and looked at Ben. "How *does* she know? Smell?"

"Yeah, she smells the milk," said Ben. "And then, Suzy, the bag is the only part of a horse that's got no hair. Maybe the babies like that, maybe they expect it, anyhow it must taste nicer than a mouthful of hair. Don't you be worrying; it won't take that filly long to find the right place."

Just then the little foal did find the bag, and planting her long legs apart, she stretched up and started her first meal. After a few pulls, she looked around at the people watching her, and Suzy was thrilled to see that the star on her forehead was just like Falada's. Ben noticed, too. "Star's the same but the color's different. I call her a real bay, don't you, Mr. Taylor?"

The star vanished as the foal turned her head and reached again toward her mother's bag and her first breakfast.

Suzy and her father walked up to the house for their breakfast. "Dad, not just because she's Falada's, but don't you think there's something special about this foal?"

Mrs. Taylor was standing in the doorway watching them as they approached. "What is it?" she called.

"Filly," said Mr. Taylor briefly.

"Oh, Jim — !"

"Mummie, don't you like girls?"

"I love them dearly," said Mrs. Taylor, bending to

kiss her own girl, "But colts can generally run faster — and this foal has got to run."

"She will, Mummie. Oh, she will! A baby that whickers the way she did before she could even get up on her feet is strong." Suzy looked at her father for confirmation but he said nothing, and a little soberly all three went into the house.

Chapter TWO

Suzy wanted to stay home from school to watch the new baby, but her parents vetoed this firmly.

"I promise I know everything they are going to teach me at school today. Please!"

"No," said her mother. "Run upstairs and wash, and put on a clean dress. Do you know your spelling?"

"Perfectly. *Sep-ar-ate* — that's the hardest. Can't I stay?" Her mother shook her head.

At school, Suzy was restless and inattentive. Her thoughts were back to the early morning, remembering a small brown head as it slowly lifted and greeted its new world with a whicker. Daddy won't say so perhaps, but if the foal had a strong voice like that, it must mean — it had to mean — she was strong all over. Strong heart, strong legs that would run fast, win big purses, pay that awful loan? Her eyes were as misty as the foal's, and Miss Crawley, her teacher, spoke to her twice before she even heard.

It was a sharp — "Susan!" — that aroused her, but then Miss Crawley smiled and said, "Suzy, your foal, like Mary's lamb, doesn't belong in school. We are studying arithmetic, not horses."

Suzy stared at the blackboard, but the figures faded mysteriously into small foals. This made it hard to understand what Miss Crawley was explaining. Finally recess came and she rushed thankfully out to the playground with the other children. Suzy and her best friend, Joan, always ate their lunch together, and they walked off now to their favorite spot under the big maple at the edge of the playground.

"Joan!" Suzy began, "the most wonderful — " and she gave a rapid account of the foal's arrival.

"I wish I'd been there. Will your father let you name the colt?"

Suzy was annoyed, and looked it, but tried to keep her voice patient. "A colt is a *boy*. This foal is a *filly*, a *girl*. I should think you'd know baby things like that."

"Why should I?" asked Joan coldly. "I hardly ever saw a horse until we moved here last fall. My father is a scientific farmer, and we have trucks and tractors, no horses."

"I'm sorry. Let's talk about names. Daddy will let me pick the name if I can think of a good enough one. I — "

The school bell interrupted, and the girls hurried to join the lines forming to march into school. The afternoon session seemed to last forever, but finally it was over, and Suzy and Joan rushed out to the bus to try to get a seat together.

Joan said, as if they'd just stopped talking, "You said you'd thought of a name."

"I have. But there are strict, hard rules about naming Thoroughbreds. For one thing, the name has to be sent to the Jockey Club and registered."

"I've never heard of the Jockey Club," Joan interrupted.

"We've heard plenty. They're the men who make all the rules about racing and things like that. They're the bosses — and you can't argue."

"I should think your father would be the boss of his own horses."

"He is, and he's not. If you want to race your horses, you have to mind the rules. And we want to race." Suzy thought with a shiver how important it was for their horses to race — and to win. It seemed funny now to think how proud she'd been of the new stable. When it was being built, she had gone every day to watch its progress. Even the timber smelled good, and she had thought with pleasure of the horses who would be stabled in it — horses getting their training and kept near the track to make it more convenient. It was all any horse — or owner — could want in the way of a stable, except for the loan her father had had to get to pay for it. That seemed to threaten everything she loved, like a storm cloud that wouldn't blow away.

"But what name did you think of?" Joan's question brought Suzy back to the bus.

"You have to think of three, and you never know

which one they'll take — or why. They don't give reasons for refusing. The name can't have more than sixteen letters. You can't have any name anyone else has. It's awful."

"You just haven't thought of one, or you'd say."

"I have so. This foal whickered the second she was born, and I want to name her Whickery. Daddy says he'll think about it, and he imagines the Jockey Club will think even harder. So I don't know."

"I bet I could think of a good name in two minutes."

"What?" Suzy was openly scornful.

Joan stared out of the bus window. "Corn Pone," she said finally, thinking of one of her favorite foods.

Suzy's laugh was high and artificial. "Breads! All the breads were used up long ago. There is a Pop-over and a Soda-Biscuit, and Salt-Rising, and all that stuff. There's a place in Albermarle County that has all the fruit and nut names. Somebody else has the spices — Cinnamon won one of the big races last year. So now do you think it's so easy?"

"No. Anyway, I think Whickery is a wonderful name. What others will you send with it?"

Suzy shook her head. She had thought of Nickery as a second choice because you could say the little filly had either whickered or nickered. But she liked Whickery better. The third name? Maybe Daddy would have an idea.

The bus slowed down for her stop, and she got up with relief. She nodded carelessly to Joan and said,

"They'll take Whickery." It made her feel better to say it, and in a minute she was off the bus and running up the long driveway to the house. She flew up the stairs to her room, barely stopping to say hello to her mother before stripping off her school dress and climbing into blue jeans and shirt. Suzy felt as if she couldn't wait one more second to see the baby. She headed at once for the small stable that Daddy called the maternity ward.

Falada and her daughter were not there now, however, but in a small paddock nearby. Daddy had explained long ago that a new mother and foal must keep to themselves for the first nine days. By that time the baby would be strong enough to keep up with the other foals in the big pasture, even to join in their game — it looked like tag — as they ran frolicking up and down the field. But if she started too young, she could easily be hurt by a pair of small flying hoofs.

When Suzy arrived at the small paddock, Ben was already there, leaning over the fence and watching mother and daughter. Suzy climbed the rail fence and perched beside him.

"How's she doing, Ben?" Her voice was anxious.

Ben cleared his throat, spat out his tobacco, and turned to look at Suzy. "Mighty frisky," he said, "that's how she's doing. Acts like she's a month old already. Now, Suzy, don't you go in there — "

But Suzy had already dropped inside the paddock from her perch atop the fence.

"Falada's going to nip you if you come too close," he warned.

"I'll be careful."

Falada had heard the soft thud as Suzy landed, and lifted her head and stared. Falada was acting, Suzy thought, as if she did not remember her, and did not care to make her acquaintance. The foal, sensing her mother's feeling, ran quickly and tried to hide, pressed closely against her mother's far side. Suzy kept very still while Falada looked her over, and then Suzy began to walk toward mare and foal. Her movements were slow — Ben warned her again that any quick motion would be alarming — but they seemed not to like her coming, and walked off. The foal remained on the far side of her mother, and all Suzy could see were four stiff, slender legs.

"You, Suzy!" Ben called, "keep away! Let Falada get used to being a mama. You pen her in a corner there, she kick you sure."

"I *know*," said Suzy crossly. "Don't act like I'm a baby. I reckon I've been around one million foals before this one."

"Not on this farm, you haven't. Come out of the paddock. I don't know which'll make your papa the maddest — if you get hurt, or Falada gets upset."

Suzy returned unwillingly and climbed the fence once more, standing now on the outside next to Ben. She stood very still and began to talk in a low, coaxing voice.

"It's Suzy, Falada. You love me, remember? See — I brought you a carrot." She put her hand in the pocket of her blue jeans, and a carrot slowly appeared.

Falada lifted her head, sniffed, took a tentative step, and stopped to look things over. After a moment, she began a slow amble in Suzy's direction. Suzy held the carrot out. Falada's nostrils quivered, she took a long step, and in a moment had the carrot and was crunching it. Suzy rubbed Falada's soft white nose. Suddenly the foal, hugged tight to her mother's shoulder, edged forward and gave Suzy a curious look. Suzy dropped to her knees and began crooning —

"Oh, you beautiful thing — you beautiful, beautiful thing —" She reached a gentle hand through the fence and tried to stroke the baby. With a jerk the little foal pulled back from the strange white hand and ran quickly behind her mother. From that safe refuge, she peeped out.

Ben laughed. "What I tell you?" he called, from his place against the fence. "Around horses as much as you are, seems like you'd know you got to be gradual. Let them get used to seeing you and smelling you, before you go touching."

"I *was* gradual, and I don't smell. Mother makes me take a bath every single day. I couldn't have a smell."

"You got a smell the same as every animal that walks on two or four feet," said Ben, and started off for the stable.

Suzy thought about this. Her father had told her

many times that while horses, of course, depend on eyes and ears, he thought it was chiefly the sense of smell that made them able to recognize people and things. "Oh, I hope I smell very strong," she thought, and resolved that when she bathed that night, at least she wouldn't use soap.

Each day, as soon as she got home from school, Suzy went down to see how Falada and the baby were thriving. Ben kept a supply of carrots at the stable, and Suzy always picked up one or two for her favorite. The baby was too young to try them — she would not even attempt grazing until she was about six weeks old — but Falada seemed to feel about carrots the way Suzy did about candy.

Suzy sat on the fence, holding out a carrot, and Falada looked her over gravely. After a long survey she walked toward the fence, her foal pressed tight to her flank. When she had eaten the treat, she stayed, as Suzy said, to talk things over and have her muzzle scratched. The little foal watched this with bright, alert eyes, and sometimes she, too, edged forward. But a sudden movement, such as a quickly outstretched hand, would send her scurrying back to her mother. The baby was still very slim, but Suzy thought her body had begun to fill out. She trotted around her small paddock, another sign of growing up, though she was careful never to get far from her mother.

All through the week, Suzy waited impatiently. On

Saturday, when she would be ten days old, Whickery was to get her first halter, and she and her mother would then be put in the big paddock with the other mares and foals. Everyone called her Whickery now, although her name would not be official until the Jockey Club confirmed it; that was the rule, Mr. Taylor reminded Suzy.

Suzy looked at her father anxiously. "But suppose we call her Whickery and they won't let us have it?"

"Then it'll be her nickname, and she'll have another, an official name. Now look," said Mr. Taylor briskly, "I know you think there's just one mare and just one foal on this farm, but actually there are sixteen, besides sixty other horses. They're all important, and I've got to see about them."

"How've the other horses been doing?" Suzy felt a guilty twinge, because she'd been so absorbed in Falada and Whickery that she'd forgotten, or almost forgotten, the other horses. Some of them were away at different tracks, and she hadn't even remembered they were running!

"Not so well," said Mr. Taylor gravely. "Funny thing, Sue, but we've been in a streak of bad luck ever since Falada had her accident. It's been a long time — " He shook his shoulders and squared them. "Well, we got into a bad period, and we'll get out of it, too."

"I wish we could just raise horses and not race them."

They were standing in the road leading to the stables, and Suzy drew a line with her sneaker in the soft white sand and looked up at her father.

"We can't — and raise Thoroughbreds. And that's all I'm interested in raising. A Thoroughbred has to prove himself, and the way he does it is by running. The other people who raise horses aren't going to take my word for it that mine are better than theirs. You, for instance, would go up in the air like a rocket if some breeder claimed to have a better mare than Falada. We have to prove what we say, and the place we show them is on the track. Satisfied?"

"Yes, sir, I reckon so. But what about that big bill, that note at the bank?" Suzy had composed herself and tried not to sound as worried as she felt.

"If we're going to have a real business conference, we'll sit on the fence." Taking his daughter's hand, Mr. Taylor walked to the fence that bounded the yearlings' paddock, and climbed to the top rail. "Now, old girl, it's like this. We had a couple of good years, we were expanding; a stable down by the track would be a great convenience, so we built it. I borrowed part of the money. Now we're having slim times, and paying back is awkward."

"What happens if we can't pay?" Suzy's throat was dry.

"We don't lose our courage." Mr. Taylor gave his daughter a reassuring pat. "We economize wherever we can. And we hope to begin winning some purses."

"I can do more than I'm doing!" Suzy hooked her toes more firmly under the fence rail. "Let me do more

than just look after Falada. Please, please! Don't say —
just study harder at school!"

"I was about to," Mr. Taylor laughed guiltily.
"There is one important thing you can do, and that's to
keep your eyes open. Feed is disappearing."

"Feed disappearing! Who would take it?"

"Well, we're pretty sure it isn't rats. They get some, of
course, but not this much."

"I'll watch. Anybody knows better than to steal. Can't
we set a trap?"

"No. You'd have to use something as big as a bear
trap, and that might break the thief's leg or arm. It's il-
legal anyway. Just keep your eyes peeled."

"Oh, I will. And I can do some more of the work,
too."

"Your mother doesn't want you at the stables all the
time, around a lot of rough-talking men. But Ben's different, and if you just stick with him, maybe she won't
mind. There are plenty of things you could give him a
hand with."

"Daddy, thank you, thank you!" Suzy jumped off the
fence and then climbed back up and gave her father a
kiss. "Now I'll feel I'm really helping to earn that old
barn. I'll go and tell Ben I'm his assistant, and not just
for Falada."

Ben wasn't in any of the different stables, the feed
room, or the tack room, so Suzy went as usual to the paddock. She pulled a carrot out of one pocket for Falada,
and an apple out of another for herself and started to

munch it. As she stood at the fence, Falada slowly ambled over, the little foal keeping pace with her and touching her side as she walked. Suzy held the carrot out, but Falada pushed it aside and neatly lifted the apple out of the surprised Suzy's fingers.

"That's *mine*," said Suzy, but too late. Falada crunched the apple, and a little of the juice ran out of her mouth. Another quick, neat motion, and she had the carrot too.

Suzy laughed and slid off the fence into the paddock. She was trying to do just as Ben said, and approach the foal almost imperceptibly. Whickery, however, guessed what she planned and ran to her mother's side and snuggled close. They played tag this way for a minute or two, and then Falada sensed that her baby was frightened and laid her ears back. Suzy scrambled to the top of the fence again just as Ben appeared.

"You teasing that foal?" he asked. "What'd I tell you — ?"

"I'm not doing one thing. Falada even stole my apple. I wouldn't tease a baby. I just wanted to hug her."

"She don't want to hug *you*," said Ben severely. "Leave her be. Look all you want to, but creeping up like that, you scare her to death."

"You *said* to creep, to go very slowly."

"I say now, leave her be, or I'll tell your papa you're making the both of them nervous. You go fill Falada's trough if you want to, and bring her feed out. Then stay on the fence. Maybe Falada don't feel so good today."

31

Suzy went to fill the trough — had Daddy already told Ben she was to be his helper? — then asked for another job when she finished.

"Nothing now. Maybe later. And leave that foal alone."

Suzy swallowed. "Just what you say, Ben." But she thought to herself, "Let Falada miss me: I'll give my carrots to Moonbeam and Moonboy for a while."

Moonbeam pricked her ears at the sound of someone approaching her paddock, and began walking toward the gate. Moonbeam was only twelve, but she had been blind for several years. Her colt had to wear a bell around his neck so that she could locate him by its sound. But Moonboy was standing very still now, and though his mother cocked her ears in different directions, she could hear nothing of him.

"He does that all the time," Ben remarked, coming up with the rations and standing beside Suzy for a minute. "That colt's a plumb devil. Seems like he just loves to tease his mama. Look at him now. He heard her whinny, but he won't answer just to fret her. You watch."

The paddock was small, and Moonbeam continued her searching, whinnying as she walked. Soon she sniffed her foal and changed her direction. Just as she got close, Moonboy gave a small leap and started toward the other side of the paddock. He was not quite quick enough. His mother gave him a small nip as he passed, and he yelped in surprise. He turned then, sidling up to his mother, and stood rubbing gently against her. She turned her head, and Suzy thought she looked reproachful. "He's a bad boy," she called to Moonbeam. "Don't just nip him — bite him hard!"

"He just wants somebody to play with," said Ben. "I reckon horses are the sociablest animals in the world. He wants to run with the other foals is all."

Suzy knew that Moonbeam had to stay in her own small paddock for her own protection, but she couldn't help feeling sorry for Moonboy, too. "Why can't Moonboy go with the other mares and foals, and just come back to Moonbeam when he's hungry?"

Ben shook his head. "You know better. Colts are born hungry. You don't put them on a schedule like a baby. He nurses whenever he feels like it. The other mares would run him off if he came nudging around them. He's got to stay right here until he's weaned, whether he likes it or not. There's lots of only children in the world." Ben smiled at Suzy. "You one, and you get on pretty good."

Suzy smiled back, but privately she thought that Ben was so old — he must be forty — that he'd forgotten how things really were. Being an only child was *lonesome*. If she didn't have Joan for a best friend — well, she had her, that was the important thing. But she understood how Moonboy felt.

A few days later, as she went with Ben on his rounds,

she said, "I wish I could give Moonbeam some extra feed for a treat, just to sort of make up to her for being blind."

"She gets all that's good for her. Feed goes too fast as it is. I wish I knew — "

"I've been watching the feed room ever since Daddy said feed was disappearing, but I never see anyone who ought not to be there. I've even watched for footprints, but there aren't any."

"Who'd leave a footprint in a lot of oats?" Ben looked at her in surprise. "You find footprints in sand or mud or something *soft*."

Suzy laughed uncomfortably. "That's right. I guess I wasn't using my head, was I? But I will from now on."

Saturday morning came, and Suzy hovered around Ben until he finally said impatiently, "What you hanging around for? Take yourself some time off. We've fed everything that needs feeding. Putting that halter on Whickery will take just one second. You've seen plenty of foals get their first halter."

Suzy stared at him. How could a grown man be so dumb? Then she said, "You know it's different. I saw Whickery when she was one minute old. Getting her halter is like being baptized — " Ben frowned at such an irreverent idea, and Suzy changed it hastily " — or the first day of school, or something big."

"Come on, then," said Ben, relenting, and pulled the tiny halter out of his pocket.

"Let me carry it?" Suzy took the small halter out of Ben's hands and looked at the brass plate on it which said FALADA. She held the halter up and laughed. "Falada! I'd like to see her get her big head in this teeny thing!"

"Whickery's really got no name of her own yet. I've heard your papa tell you a hundred times. Well, we got to know which foal is which, don't we? So we put the dam's name on the foal's halter. It's only sense."

"Yes, I reckon so," said Suzy absently, rubbing the brass plate. "Ben, I've got a pin. Is it all right if I scratch WHICKERY below FALADA?"

Ben grinned. "I got no objection to scratching; fact is, I like it fine for myself. You sit there on the fence and see what you can do, and I'll be back this way in five minutes."

Suzy sat on the top rail with her feet hooked on the one below, and went to work. The pin skidded on the highly polished surface, and before she knew quite how it happened she was holding a pin so bent it looked like a fish hook, and there were just a few meaningless scratches on the brass.

"I could have told you," said Ben, coming up and looking at the bent pin. "I could have told you, but you wouldn't have believed me. Folks just have to find out things for themselves. Now let's get this halter on."

"Ben, could I, could I — ?" Suzy looked at him hopefully. "You know I'm supposed to help you."

"No sirree," said Ben firmly. "What're we putting this

35

halter on for, anyway? Answer me that."

"You just said — so we don't get her mixed up."

"An-nd, so she gets used to being handled. If the first time anybody puts a hand on her it's not done right, or she gets scared, we'll have trouble with her. This is a job for experts — and I'm the expert."

"O.K.," said Suzy, with only a small sigh. "I'll be an expert someday."

Falada was none too pleased when Suzy and Ben walked into the paddock. She began to edge off. The foal ran around to the far side and nestled against her mother, trying to hide. Ben walked straight up to Falada, talking coaxingly. "Come on, girl — come on, pretty — " His voice seemed to reassure Falada. She stood quietly and let him scratch her glossy neck, and soon the foal peeped out curiously to see what was going on. She edged up to Ben and began to sniff his coat. He stood very still until the baby tried to crowd her nose into his coat pocket. With a quick movement, Ben's arm was around her neck, holding it still. With another deft motion, the halter was over Whickery's head before she knew what had happened. Ben fastened the buckle and stroked her. "That's a good baby," he said, "that's a good girl," but Whickery trembled slightly and ran behind her mother the minute Ben let her go.

She pressed close to Falada's warm body and tried to rub the halter off. Falada, who didn't like the feeling of the leather, and especially of the brass buckle, turned her head and looked inquiringly at her daughter.

Whickery paid no attention and rubbed all the harder. Falada moved off, but the little foal followed closely, rubbing as she walked. Falada switched her tail in disgust and finally gave her baby a tentative nip. Whickery jumped and ran off — then, with a sudden change of mood, ran up and down the paddock.

"She's just found out she can run," said Ben. "Way she's acting, you'd think she's the only foal that knows how. Look at those heels!"

Whickery was really running, giving little bucking jumps, her heels high in the air.

"She's so beautiful," sighed Suzy. "Do you think she minds her halter much?"

"Look at those heels!" Ben repeated. "She's not studying about her halter. She's kicking up her heels because she feels so good. It don't take two minutes for foals to get used to halters. Then they forget all about them, or think they're part of them, like their manes and tails. Your clothes don't worry you; you don't think about them. Whickery's like you, only she don't fret about colors."

Ben laughed, pleased with his joke, and Suzy could think of nothing to say. How did he know she was always wanting pink or red, and that Mother wouldn't let her wear it because of her red hair? At this moment, Whickery trotted up and sniffed inquisitively at Suzy.

"You know you're mine!" Suzy cried delightedly, but at the sound of her voice, Whickery rushed away again and hid behind her mother.

Chapter THREE

ANOTHER WEEK SLIPPED AWAY on the sweet spring winds, and Suzy and Joan sat in school smiling at each other. Friday afternoon! It was the very best time of all, Suzy thought, with school temporarily over and the weekend just ahead, like a lovely, uncut cake. Joan was coming to spend the night and they'd do — well, everything.

Joan's overnight bag was in the coat closet, and the minute school was out the two girls seized the bag and, swinging it between them, rushed out to the bus. "Did you bring your blue jeans?" Suzy asked. "Daddy says you can ride one of the lead ponies if you want to."

"Yes, they're in there." The girls were seated in the school bus, and Joan leaned down and patted her bag. "What's the pony's name, and what are you going to ride?"

"I'm riding Elsinore and you'll have Sir Knight. He's not really a pony; the exercise boys just call him that. Dad says lead ponies are just as necessary in training racers as people are. He's light-colored so the others can see him easily — "

They were still talking horses as they went into the house, and Mrs. Taylor, who heard them, went to the top of the stairs and called, "Neigh-h-h!"

"Oh, Mother, that's not funny! Why can't you just say, 'Hello'?"

"From the conversation, I thought I was talking to a couple of ponies. What are you girls going to do?"

Suzy looked amazed. "DO? We're going right out to the paddocks and then we're going riding. Joan is going to try Sir Knight."

"Did Daddy say that was all right? I know you haven't ridden much, Joan," Mrs. Taylor added apologetically, "and Suzy's been riding something or other since she was about five. Don't let her overpersuade you."

"Oh no, ma'am, she isn't. The last two times I was here, Ben put me up and led me around, and *he* said I was ready to try it alone now."

"Well, if Ben says so — "

Suzy had darted off to her room to change into riding things, and now stuck her head out of the door impatiently. "Come on, Joan," she called.

Joan, who was using her company manners, continued talking, in a very put-on, grown-up way, Suzy thought. "Thank you for letting me come, Mrs. Taylor — "

"Stop being so polite and get your jeans on," Suzy

said as soon as the bedroom door was safely shut. Two minutes later they were running across the lawn toward the paddock. There was a drainage ditch at the edge of the field, which they jumped, and then both climbed the rail for a look around.

"I can walk this fence," said Joan, and proceeded to do so, but Suzy would not be diverted.

"There they are!" she said, pointing toward the edge of the big pasture. And there against the sky line of the gently rising field were the sixteen mothers and their babies.

The mares were all grazing peacefully, most of them facing the same way, their noses down wind, so they could smell any approach. The foals were running around, playing their game of tag, nipping each other gently, and then all tearing off to one end of the huge twenty-acre field. In another minute they had run back, but Suzy looked anxious. "I don't see Whickery."

"I see one baby just peeping out from behind its mother."

"*That's* Whickery," said Suzy, relief in her voice.

Whickery was the youngest of the foals and had been in the pasture with her mother not quite a week. She was like a new child at school; the others were interested but not yet sure they wanted to play with her. As the girls watched, Whickery sidled up to a foal who moved off at once. She tried still another, and this one gave her a slight nip. Whickery whinnied and ran straight to her mother, who raised a watchful head.

41

Whickery pressed close and after a moment reached for her mother's bag and had a consoling drink.

"Look how she braces her legs," said Joan. "They're as stiff as — as stiff as — "

"Stilts," Suzy supplied, and Joan laughed. They edged up slowly as they talked, and Suzy began murmuring consoling words to Whickery, whose head had reappeared. "Pretty baby, pretty baby," she said, stretching out her hand to the foal which looked at her with bright, alert eyes. "Do they treat you mean? Won't they let you play?" She took a step closer, but Whickery tossed her pretty head and ran around to her mother's other side.

One after the other, the mares lifted their heads to see what was going on. After a moment Falada started toward the girls, with Whickery close at her side, and a few seconds later, as if she had given a signal, the other mares started too. They came from every corner of the field and slowly surrounded Suzy and Joan until they seemed the hub of a great wheel of horses. Some of the foals stood by their mothers; the older and bolder tried to force their way closer.

Joan gripped Suzy. "Those mares are awfully big," she said in a low voice as if afraid they might overhear. "Why do they all want to come up to us at once? I wish they'd go away."

"Are you scared?" Suzy could hardly believe it. "Mares won't hurt you unless you start teasing their foals. They're just sociable. They want to talk to us. And

I guess they hope we've brought them something good, like carrots." She slapped her pockets regretfully. She had been in such a hurry to get to the paddock that she had forgotten all about bringing treats.

The mares began sniffing the two girls, running their noses up and down their thin cotton shirts, and trying to force a big mouth into a small pocket. Suzy was used to this and loved it. She began stroking Falada gently. The long, whiskery hairs on Falada's nose trembled slightly. She liked the soft massage and held out her head for more.

Joan tried to shrink back as a big black mare began sniffing her, but there was no place to go. Wherever she looked, a mare's long face looked back at her, big nostrils sniffed her, and large soft lips ran over her clothes and face. "Sue!" she cried in a strangled voice, "they're all around us. We're in the middle. We can't get out."

"Who wants to?"

"We can't get out!" Joan repeated desperately. She had turned very pale and was almost crying.

"We can so." Suzy began to talk, no longer coaxingly, but firmly. "Go along," she said to Falada who was closest, and gave her a slight slap on the shoulder. "Get along with you! Go see about your business!" She slapped her again harder.

Falada lifted her head from Suzy's shoulder and turned away with dignity. The other mares stopped sniffing and lifted their heads. Suzy, distributing small slaps and orders, urged them on. Slowly they all turned and started for the rising ground of the field, and in a moment or two were grazing peacefully again, their foals beside them and the girls forgotten.

Joan, whose color had returned to normal, cleared her throat and said defensively, "I wasn't really scared. I just wondered — "

Suzy started to laugh, and said, "Not scared!" but decided she was being mean. After all, horses were a very new experience to Joan. "Do you want to ride now?" she asked by way of changing the subject. Joan nodded, and they started for the tack room where the saddles and bridles were hanging in neat rows. "We'll saddle up. I do it, now that we've let one of the stable boys go."

"Can you really do it? I know a girl whose saddle slid right under the horse because she couldn't pull the girth tight enough. She was in the saddle, and slid round with it, and there she was hanging upside down!"

"I can pull a girth tight, and besides, Ben always checks. We'll get the horses saddled and then he'll come fussing around. You'll see."

"Saddling's fun," said Joan, tugging at a buckle. "I'd always want to saddle my own horse."

"I always wanted to, too. But when I was smaller, I wasn't tall enough to throw the saddle over a horse, and Ben didn't like it if the saddle or bridle even touched the floor. He wants to keep this tack room like a parlor."

Ben appeared, as Suzy had predicted, and checked

their work. "Who let this saddle drag in the dirt?" he asked. "I'll have to put you young ladies to cleaning tack, to teach you to be more careful."

"Not now, please, Ben, not now! We want to ride."

Ben said no more but held out his hand. Suzy put her foot in it and jumped lightly into the saddle. Joan hung back a little, and Ben asked, "You want me to lift you on?"

Joan nodded, and in a moment she was mounted, too. Ben checked the length of the stirrups, looked at the bridles to see if they were comfortable, and then asked, "Where you going?"

"To the track first, and then we'll just roam around."

"Not too far. Remember what your papa said. And don't go faster than a trot. Joan's got to get used to things."

"O.K., O.K.," said Suzy, in order not to hear any more advice. She pressed her heels into Elsinore's sides, and he moved off. Better get out of Ben's range, Suzy thought, or he'd use all their riding time telling them what not to do. He didn't realize how soon she'd have to be back for the evening chores. She wanted to do them; it gave her a good feeling to know she was a real help. Ben and her father both said she was. Since Sully's dismissal, she had taken over part of his work — enough to make a real difference, Ben said. This afternoon, though, was one of the times when helping was a nuisance. She would have loved to ride all around the farm with Joan and not bother about the feeding and watering. With a small sigh, she called to Joan to get started.

Sir Knight, with Joan looking rather timid, moved up beside her. The girls walked their horses down the driveway and crossed the highway to the fields which lay on the other side, talking as they went. There were two tracks laid out here: a smaller, covered one for winter, and the big one where the real training of the racers took place.

"Nine furlongs," said Suzy professionally, pausing to survey it.

"There are only eight in a mile," objected Joan. "The arithmetic book says so."

Suzy had been hoping for that. "Some of the biggest races are a mile and an eighth. That's *nine* furlongs. That's why Daddy had the track built this way. Our horses are in plenty of big races — and they win them, too," she added proudly, and then fell silent. The races they had been winning lately were few indeed. Suzy had seen her father looking graver and more worried, and he and her mother seemed to have many serious conversations. She had come in on the end of one such talk before they had seen her.

"Nobody wins all the time," her father was saying. "You can't expect it. But the horses have had a phenomenal number of colds. And then losing Water Boy of pneumonia was a bad break. It seems to me that we can't turn them out into the paddock without one of them pulling a tendon and getting laid up for six weeks — " But when he saw Suzy he stopped at once and said, "Hi, scooter," and was out the door before she could question him.

"Suzy!" called Joan, and Suzy came out of her thoughts and turned to her. "I called you three times and you never heard."

"I was just thinking. What did you want?"

"This track now, is it just like a real track?"

The track circled in a big sandy oval, and Suzy looked at it with pride. "It is a real track," she said. "We could have races here. The sand is to cushion the horses' feet. Daddy says a Thoroughbred's ankle is as dainty as a real lady's. You watch a horse running, and if it has to pound on hard ground, it can break the little bones in the ankle. Dad says — "

"When are we going to ride around the track?" Joan was impatient, and Suzy laughed and said, "I reckon I do sound like a teacher. But don't you want to know *everything*?"

"I want to ride," said Joan, and started to trot down the track. Suzy followed and in a moment passed her as Elsinore broke into a canter. Sir Knight started to canter too, and then to run.

"Hold him in!" Suzy shouted, and Joan pulled hard on the reins. Sir Knight usually set the pace on the track, and it was hard work to pull him down. Finally he went into a slow canter, and Joan grinned at Suzy. "That was fun."

"Don't do it again. Not until you're experienced. Dad

says he thinks you're going to have a good, natural seat — but anybody needs practice."

"Did he really say that?" Joan was pleased and, pressing her heels into Sir Knight's sides, cantered again. Suzy caught up and came alongside just as Joan, a little rattled, dug her heels sharply into her mount. Sir Knight, not used to this, gave a little buck which caught Joan off guard. She flew out of the saddle and over his head, landing on the soft earth of the track, and sat there a moment, looking surprised and scared. Suzy rode quickly up to her.

"What happened? Are you hurt?"

"My seat hurts. I don't know what happened. I was starting to canter and then — well, then I was here!" Joan stood, then rubbed the seat of her blue jeans softly.

"If you're all right, we'll catch Sir Knight and get you on him before anybody finds out what happened."

"I've ridden enough for today," said Joan.

Suzy decided not to argue and turned Elsinore's head toward the green middle of the track where Sir Knight, reins trailing on the ground, was eating with relish the lespedeza, a Japanese clover with which the field was sown. Suzy slid out of her saddle, and, reins over her arm, started toward Sir Knight. Joan joined her, but each time they came close, Sir Knight lifted his head from the succulent clover and moved a few paces away.

"We'll *never* catch him," said Joan despairingly after five minutes or so of this, and continuing to give her seat a gentle rub.

"Pick a bunch of this lespedeza," Suzy finally said, "and hold it out to him. He seems to think it's ice cream and cake all in one. If he grabs the lespedeza, I'll grab him."

And that was the way it worked out. Sir Knight stretched to get the bunch of green held temptingly before him, Suzy made a quick dive for the trailing reins, and Sir Knight was captured before he knew it.

"How'll you get on?" Joan asked.

Suzy pointed to the rail fence and, with the reins of a horse over each arm, walked toward it. Joan followed slowly and said, "It's funny, but I feel just like walking instead of riding. I'll just lead Sir Knight back to the stable."

Suzy was not taken in by this. "It's a rule, if you fall, you have to mount again right away or you'll lose your nerve. You won't fall any more. We won't gallop. I'll help you mount. Keep your legs straight and keep them close to Sir Knight, and don't kick him."

Joan looked at Sir Knight a long minute. Suzy remembered some of her own early falls and knew just how Joan was feeling. "Sir Knight didn't mean to hurt you. He wasn't expecting you to kick him that way, and that's why he bucked. He won't do it again. You climb the fence and drop into the saddle while I hold the reins." Joan did as directed, and Suzy gave her an encouraging smile. "You're all right. You want to walk Sir Knight or trot?"

"Walk," said Joan. Her usually pink cheeks had paled again after the experience of the afternoon, but her hands on the reins were steady. The horses, who knew they were headed for home, accelerated their walk until it became a trot and then a gentle canter. Suzy was proud of Joan who no longer looked frightened, but seemed to be enjoying herself. They paused at the hitching rack and Ben appeared. Suzy slid out of the saddle unassisted, but Ben gave Joan a hand.

"I was over near the track and I saw you go flying out of your saddle like an apple somebody throwed," he said. "You hurt?"

Joan shook her head. Suzy looked anxious. "Ben, are you going to tell?"

Ben laughed. "I'm going to tell those horses to take better care of you next time." He gave Sir Knight an affectionate smack. The girls exchanged guilty smiles and then announced that they were ready to help with the evening feeding.

"Come along with me then," said Ben. "Joan, you want to measure the oats — and Suzy, you go in the stalls and put them in the troughs."

"Are oats still disappearing, Ben?"

Ben's brow furrowed. "They are for a fact. I can't seem to catch whatever or whoever is taking them. I set me a few traps of different kinds, but no results."

"I keep an eye out every time I go for the feed," said Suzy, "and I just tiptoe to the door, hoping I'll catch the thief. But suppose it's a man instead of a rat or whatever animal likes oats?"

"A man would have a right hard time getting to the oats, what with the night watchman making the rounds every hour." Ben stopped forking the clean hay into a stall and looked at Suzy as if he'd heard all he wanted about oats.

"It wouldn't be hard for a man who'd worked on the place and knew just when Clarence went around."

"You maybe got something I hadn't thought of," said Ben, scratching his head, "and I'll get my mind to it. Man or not, I'm going to catch whoever is taking them. But get on with the feeding now. The filly in that end stall acts like she's going to kick the wall down if she don't get her supper."

The hammering hoofs quieted as Suzy entered with her pail.

Chapter FOUR

Suzy had the feeling that if she could keep Whickery still long enough, she would actually see her grow. She was six weeks old now and at least two hands taller and thirty pounds heavier than at birth. And she was about to get her own rations.

"We'll fix a place for her in the creep," Ben told Suzy, and they went off together to the big pasture. The creep was a bit of the pasture enclosed by a fence made of a single rail. Its name came from the fact that the rail was high enough for the foals to creep in and out easily, but low enough to keep out the mares.

"I think it's awful for the mares to be so greedy that they'll take their own children's food," said Suzy.

Ben just grunted. "They aren't studying about being greedy. They see some food, they're going to eat it, is all. All the creatures except folks are like that, and some folks are. We'll put Whickery's trough here and show it to her, but I don't reckon the big boys will let her keep it."

Ben set the small wooden trough down and filled it with the sweet feed, the cracked corn and molasses, oats and alfalfa, that all foals love. "I'll go catch Whickery and show her the creep," said Suzy. "This is a good time, with none of the other foals here."

Catching Whickery was hard. She played a sort of blindman's buff, slipping first from one side of her mother to the other, and Suzy, out of breath, decided to change her tactics. She ignored Whickery and, turning to Falada, pulled a carrot out of her pocket and offered it. Falada approached at once, Suzy relinquished the carrot, slipped her hand through Falada's halter, and started for the creep. Whickery followed. Like all foals, she never liked to get far from her mother, and too, she wanted to see what was going on. When they reached the creep, Whickery walked under the rail as if she had planned to all the time, and soon was sniffing around the trough.

"Stay where you are," Ben called softly. So Suzy stood outside, gently scratching Falada's neck.

Whickery started to turn away, thought better of it, bent down, and took a bite. She chewed slowly, looking off into the distance, went off — and came back to the trough for another big bite.

Suzy was almost prancing with excitement. "Isn't she smart?" she called in a stage whisper to Ben, but Ben held up a warning finger. "Let her get used to it," he said. But Whickery didn't seem to need much prac-

55

tice, for she took big mouthfuls and looked around with evident pleasure.

Suzy relaxed her grasp on Falada, who wandered toward one of the troughs for mares set outside the creep. The troughs were all empty, so Falada drifted toward a big block of rock salt and took a meditative lick. There were a dozen or so of these blocks set around the pasture, sculptured into odd shapes by the frequent licking of the mares' rough tongues.

While Suzy was watching Falada, several other foals entered the creep, and the biggest of them went over and gave Whickery a nudge. Whickery stood still, and the other foal immediately gave her a sharp nip. Whickery squealed and moved off, and the other foal at once began eating the sweet food.

"Oh, the meanie!" Suzy cried, and rushed over to run him off, but Ben spoke, "Whoa there! Whickery's got to fight this out for herself, and she will, too, in another month. Her mama's the boss of all the mares, and Whickery will boss the foals. You'll see."

"How — ?"

"She'll start running the others off from anything she wants. If they don't like it, she'll fight. If she's a good fighter, they won't mess around her. I saw Falada work up from being the mare all the others picked on, to being the boss. It was just like the spelling matches they had when I was at school. If you could outspell a boy, you moved up and took his place. We all had our places and knew them, and that's the way it is with the

mares. Falada's number 1, Annie Girl is number 2, and Heather's number 16. That's nothing against Heather. She'd rather be peaceful and pushed around, if she's got to be, to be peaceful."

"I want Whickery to be number 1."

"You can't make her. She's got to do it herself. Leave her be till she's ready." He turned to go and met Mr. Taylor coming in at the gate.

"How's Whickery doing?" he asked.

"Fine, fine. Seems like she was born knowing things. We hardly have to teach her."

"And how's your stable boy?" Mr. Taylor asked, smiling at his daughter.

"She was born knowing a lot, too. She's a good worker, a real help to me."

A pleasurable glow ran all through Suzy and came out in a grateful smile for Ben. "Ben thinks Whickery is the best thing we've got on the place," she said.

"Too early to say yet," said her father, "though she certainly looks promising. Those legs are going to be powerful." He ran a professional hand over the foal's withers and down her trembling forelegs. "Well, we need some good news around here. What we get from the tracks is bad enough. We haven't had a first in a month of Sundays."

"Daddy — "

"Sue, I *order* you not to worry," said Mr. Taylor with a look at his daughter's anxious face. "That's horse racing for you. You have a long, dry spell, and then you have some good luck that makes you forget all about it. We've had some good luck before and we'll have it again. And I think this little girl is going to bring us some." He gave Whickery an affectionate pat on the rump and left the field.

"Mr. Taylor!" Ben called. Mr. Taylor turned back.

"Oats have started disappearing fast again. I had the watchman go his rounds in reverse, trying to catch up with whoever is taking them."

"You're positive it's not rats?"

"It's a rat on two feet," said Ben. "I'm sure of that now."

"Catch him then," said Mr. Taylor impatiently. "We can't afford this kind of steady loss. You know what they say about the dripping of water wearing away stone."

He went on to his office in the stable and Suzy and Ben continued with the feeding. Suddenly Suzy stopped short. "Look, Ben." She pointed to a burned-out match lying on the ground. Ben picked it up, his face darkening with anger.

"Your papa's told these boys, I've told them, 'Just strike one match around the stables, and your job's gone.' We're not taking any chances with fire and burning up some of the best horseflesh in the country. I find that boy, I'll wring his neck."

"What would stable boys be doing over here? You and I feed the foals and mares."

"We do for a fact!" said Ben. "But one of the boys could have passed this way."

59

"Maybe the person taking the oats threw the match. It's on his way."

Ben shook his head. "Wouldn't be that big a fool. If he struck a match, the light might give him away."

"Well, what *do* you think then?" Suzy cried impatiently.

"I don't know what I think," said Ben, slipping the match into the back pocket of his overalls. "You finish the feeding. I'm going to line up every exercise boy and every stable boy on the place, show them this match, and about kill the one that lit it."

"Let me go with you! I found the match."

"You go on with the feeding," Ben repeated. "We don't want these foals hungry. And the way I'm going to talk to those boys your mama wouldn't like you to hear."

Suzy sighed and picked up her bucket, and Ben strode off toward the training track where most of the boys were likely to be. She waited impatiently all morning for Ben to reappear. When she finally found him it was afternoon, and he shook his head. "None of them knew a thing," he said. "You just keep your eye out for more matches."

That evening when Suzy went on her rounds with Ben, she saw that a small trough for Whickery had been placed in the stall beside Falada's.

She smiled. "Isn't that nice! It's just like Mummie and me having a meal together."

"Not just exactly," said Ben, smiling, too. "I never heard anybody had to tie up your mama to keep her from eating your share." As he spoke, he clipped a short strap to Falada's halter and fastened the other end to a ring in the wall. "That'll keep Miss Greedy's mouth out of what it's got no business in."

Chapter FIVE

Suzy CONTINUED TO WATCH for matches but found no more. The oats still disappeared, not in large quantities, but steadily. Mr. Taylor had the two big farm dogs unleashed and allowed to roam at night, hoping they would challenge any intruder. Sometimes Suzy would be awakened by their barking, which sounded lonely and frightening in the still country night. She'd ask the watchman next morning what had aroused the dogs, but it never turned out to be anything more exciting than another dog which had wandered over, or perhaps a weasel or fox. The watchman, as determined as Suzy to catch the thief, tried many ways of going his rounds. If the thief knew he usually started at the stable near the house, well, he'd fool him and begin near the track. That way he might catch the prowler in the oat room at a time he thought was safe.

Meanwhile the work of the farm had to go forward. There were twenty two-year-olds stabled in what Suzy always thought of as the Black Barn (because of the mortgage) down near the training tracks. Younger horses at another stage of their training were stabled elsewhere, and last year's foals, who were now called weanlings, were in the paddocks and stables near the house.

Spring was only a memory and summer well along when Ben said to Suzy one morning, "Where's that Joan that used to be over here so much? Why don't you go spend two-three days with her?"

"She's gone to camp," Suzy sighed. "Why do you want me away?"

"I don't want you grieving around here. We're going to wean the foals this week and you won't like it."

"Whickery's too young!" cried Suzy indignantly. "She's just six months. Why does Daddy — ?"

"Ask him. He's the boss. If he says 'wean,' I'm going to wean."

Suzy could hardly wait for her father to come in at lunch time so she could question him. "Why?" she began, "why do — ?"

Mr. Taylor settled into a comfortable chair on the big screened porch, and pulled Suzy to him. "Now, young lady," he said, "a few facts: This is a stock farm. If we're breeders, we've got to breed. We have a lot of brood mares, and we'd like each of them to have a foal every year. It doesn't always work out that well, but that's what we aim for. Falada's been bred, and she'll have a new foal next spring. So-o, it's better for Falada not to nurse Whickery too long. Whickery's a big girl now. She's had her own rations since she was six weeks old, and it's time her mother had a rest."

Suzy made herself walk upstairs slowly, but when she got there she threw herself on her bed. Of course, Falada ought to have a rest, but poor Whickery! She wouldn't understand. Suzy remembered from other years how upset the mothers and foals were at weaning time.

That afternoon she went with Ben and two or three helpers to round up the sixteen foals. As they were caught, a lead rein was attached to each halter, and Suzy took Whickery's. "Where are we going, Ben?" she asked.

"A far piece. We're going to get these babies as far from their mothers as we can, so they don't hear each other calling so plain. We'll take them to the little pasture down by the creek, and we'll put the mothers on the other side of the hill."

This was their first separation from their mothers, and already the foals were feeling nervous. Some of them turned their heads for a backward look at the familiar paddock, and one or two whinnied softly. Suzy walked close to Whickery, an arm around her neck, talking consolingly to her as they went.

"In three days you'll forget," she said. "Ben says so. You'll hardly remember your mother if you see her!"

But in her bed that night, Suzy barely slept. She heard the anguished whinnying of the foals, and the mothers'

64

mournful cries in answer. It went on all night, and all next day, and the next night, too, though then the cries were not so frequent. The third night, everyone slept better, and the morning after that, when Suzy went to the creek paddock, the foals were cropping the grass peacefully, and one or two were already running around and kicking up their heels.

To mark their new status, the foals were no longer called foals but "weanlings," and they were separated into two groups. The fillies were put together in a paddock not far from the stables. The colts had their own large pasture several fields away.

One hot morning, Suzy woke early. She tossed on her bed for a while, and then decided to dress and go outdoors. She pulled on her thinnest shirt and shorts, and slipped barefooted down the stairs. She opened the front door cautiously so that it wouldn't squeak, and in a moment was outside in the dewy morning. There was a pearl of moisture on every grass blade, and Suzy walked on them gently, wiggling her toes in the coolness and feeling better already. In the big elm at the corner of the house, some birds were singing — thrushes, maybe? — and from the clump of shrubbery at the edge of the lawn came a song she guessed was a blackbird's. A bobwhite whistled from the paddock, and she started toward the sound, hoping to see both him and the horses. She climbed the fence and looked down at the weanlings. Like the older horses, they were

now left out all night, except in what Ben called "falling weather." Most of the weanlings were grazing, but one or two still lay on the ground asleep.

Suzy dropped gently from the top rail of the fence into the pasture, and walked softly toward the middle of the field. Two of the fillies lay stretched out sleeping, while the others continued to crop the grass around them. Whickery was one of the sleepers, and Suzy was almost beside her before she opened a questioning eye. Suzy dropped to her knees at once and began to stroke and pet her. "Don't wake up," she said. "Go back to sleep, and I'll nap with you."

Whickery half raised up, craned her neck around to see what was going on in the paddock, then lay back again and relaxed. Suzy half sat, half lay beside her, her red curls tossed against Whickery's dark mane, one hand rhythmically scratching Whickery's long, proud neck. Suzy was sure Whickery had gone back to sleep, but she herself seemed to have flopped on an anthill. She could stand it no longer and hopped to her feet. Whickery jumped up, too, gave herself a thorough shake, and rushed down to the far end of the field. In a moment, she was back, and with the other weanlings she began to drift toward the gate. Suzy turned and saw Ben standing there. "Let's feed them out here this morning," she called.

"You, Suzy, you know better," he tossed her two lead reins. "You bring in the first two and I'll come along for the next."

"You've got to go and get your breakfast," Suzy said to Whickery, fastening the lead rein to her halter. "You can come out again, but mean old Ben is going to make you stay inside for an hour or so."

"You got no call to say I'm mean," said Ben. "These fillies have got to be so used to being handled, they don't even notice it. How are they going to win races if they're scared of folks? Leave them out in the pasture all the time and they'll be as wild as birds."

Suzy had to agree. If Whickery was going to win races — and she certainly was! — there were lots of things she must learn.

"Look how tall Whickery is now," Ben continued. "Must be eleven or twelve hands."

Suzy looked at her own hands reflectively and then at Whickery. She was only six months old but she was taller than Sue already. Tired of standing, Whickery sidled over to Sue and began nibbling around her pockets. Whenever she found an apple or carrot there, she pulled it out with her strong white teeth. But this morning there was nothing, and she drew back disappointed.

"I'm sorry. I forgot." Suzy scratched Whickery's ears in apology and stroked the shaggy coat. "When is she going to lose this baby hair?"

"Not so long now," said Ben. "Give her time. She's still a baby even if she is weaned. By the time she's a year, she'll have as pretty a bay coat as you'll want to see. Get her into her stall now and let her have her breakfast." He gave Whickery a small slap, and she and Suzy started off briskly for the stable.

They had gone only a few paces when Ben called, "Wait a minute. Tell me one thing. How careful are you being about measuring the oats? You sure you're not giving some of your favorites extra helpings?"

"Of course I don't," said Suzy indignantly. "Why would you go thinking a thing like that?"

"Those oats." Ben shook his head. "I'm downright scared to tell your papa we're low on them so soon again."

The next morning, when Suzy went out to the stables, she found a very glum Ben.

"That fellow was here last night," he said. "He didn't get one oat, but he was here. Five minutes after he'd left the oat room, the watchman came back — seems he had a feeling. Clarence is as sharp as a fox but he didn't see anything and he didn't hear anything. He stood listening, and when he turned to go he thought he saw something move. He put his flashlight on, and there was that big lilac clump moving, though there wasn't a breath of wind. He started for the clump but just then he heard a commotion in the stable, and he flashed his light over there to see what was going on. That only took a second, but it was a second too many. Whoever it was, was gone."

"I think he was crazy to turn his head even for a second," Suzy said.

"He thought something might be after the horses. They're more important than oats. He feels as bad as you and me — maybe worse."

Chapter SIX

A FEW MORNINGS LATER Suzy found another match. Ben took it almost sullenly. "Looks like that fellow is trying to insult me as well as steal our oats," he said.

"I still don't understand why the dogs don't bark. They make plenty of noise about everything else."

"Because he's somebody they know," said Ben. "I got that much figured out. I'm naming no names, but you can't tell me it's not some fellow who's worked on the place the last couple of years. That's the only way they'd know the dogs well enough to get by. This fellow probly comes sneaking in, petting and coaxing the dogs, maybe giving each of them a bone, and I wouldn't be surprised if they escorted him right to the oat bin."

Suzy laughed. "You know you don't think that. Please give me just a hint who you suspect."

"Can't do it. Got nothing on him I can prove. Just a feeling. But I'll catch him if it's my last act."

"How?"

"I'm not telling because I don't know. But I'll get him." Ben stalked off to continue the feeding, the very set of his shoulders showing his state of mind.

September came. Joan returned from camp, and Suzy's thoughts were occupied by school as well as by the mystery of the missing oats. Both girls thought the work in their new grade was much harder, and the new teacher awfully strict. Suzy thought enviously of Whickery, who still had nearly a year of freedom before her. Whickery had fun on her mind, not lessons.

She raced around the pasture with the other weanlings, giving little bucking jumps as she ran. Sometimes she grazed quietly, almost nose to nose with her best friend, Cherry, a gray with black hairs running through her coat and a clump of them forming a dark star on her forehead. Though she had watched carefully, Suzy could not have said just when or how Whickery and Cherry had become friends. The weanling fillies were always together in the same pasture or stable, frolicking together, romping together; and then, before anyone realized what had happened, they were all paired off. It couldn't have been on any one special day.

Suzy stood watching them one morning while waiting for the school bus. "Don't they ever have any threesomes?" she asked Ben who happened to be passing by.

"Mighty rare. If we had nine fillies, say, instead of ten, one pair might let the odd one in. They don't want to much, but a horse is just plain sociable, and they've got to have friends. Mope, if they don't. Take Hester's foal. She was the littlest, they all picked on her, but she kept hanging around and finally they took her in. She was what you might call a second-best friend — not like you and Joan, but like that little freckled-faced girl you bring over sometimes."

Suzy nodded. Kate was all very well, but nothing to Joan. She hung on the fence for a last look before starting down the driveway for the school bus. Whickery had stopped eating and had arched her neck over Cherry's and was slowly rubbing it back and forth.

Ben followed her gaze and laughed. "Whickery just wants a good scratch. A horse's spine is kind of knobby, and it's a good place to rub against if you don't happen to have a pair of hands to scratch with. Cherry'll get her turn. You watch."

"I can't. I hear the bus blowing right now." Suzy tore down the drive.

The months slipped by, and Suzy could hardly realize Christmas had come and gone until she heard someone speak of Whickery as a yearling. It was hard to realize that the baby was a baby no longer. Whickery stood ten hands tall now, which made her the tallest of the fillies, and about as tall as the colts. Ben guessed her weight at about seven hundred pounds. She had done a lot of growing since that early spring morning when, a newborn foal, she lay on the floor of her mother's stall and let out her first confident whicker.

One of the things Suzy thought really unfair was the

system of reckoning horses' birthdays. Here was Whickery, actually just nine months old, but officially a year. She knew the rule; every Thoroughbred is one year old on the first of the January following his birth, no matter whether he was born the previous January or the previous April or May.

"Those are the rules, Sue," her father said, not patiently, and for the tenth time, when she went to him about it.

"I don't think it's fair cheating Whickery out of her birthday." Suzy looked defiant.

"She's not cheated. Like the Queen of England, she has an official birthday which happens not to be the day she was born. Whickery doesn't care. When the real day comes, give her some extra feed if you like and call it a party." He would say no more, and Suzy went off muttering.

She ran into Ben, who was all smiles. "I got me an idea about the thief. But don't say a word to your papa until we know."

"Oh Ben, who?"

"The fellow this belongs to." He held up a half-empty package of cigarettes.

"Everybody smokes." Suzy felt deflated. "You'd never find out from that."

"Not everybody smokes filter tips. And of the four men I'm thinking about, one chews tobacco and one smokes a pipe. I'll go visiting tonight and find out a thing or two."

"Well — ! Tell me the first thing tomorrow?"

"You'll know. If I'm right, I'll come to work with the sheriff and a pair of handcuffs all fixed and ready. And I'll have the key."

Suzy grinned happily. Daddy had explained that the loss of the oats would neither make nor break them. "But it's like a leak, Sue. Leaks get bigger; you lose more and more. If this fellow continues to get away with the little thefts, he'll get bolder and start on bigger things. Maybe even farm equipment. That's why it's so important to catch him."

Suzy wished she were in Ben's shoes, with evidence tucked away in her pocket. It would be wonderful to be the one to stop the leak. She thought a visit to Whickery might cheer her up so she started for the paddock.

Now that Whickery was no longer a weanling but a yearling, plans were being made for her training. Like everything else connected with horses, this would begin slowly and gently. Actually, the yearlings were between fourteen and eighteen months old when their first lessons began.

Before the training could start, the blacksmith had to pay a visit, and Suzy asked Joan over to see the shoeing. The blacksmith had hardly parked his truck in the stable yard before the two girls were peering into the back.

"Look at those rows of shoes hanging up," said Joan. "It looks like a shoe store."

"That's what it is," said the blacksmith. "Now can I fit either of you young ladies with a nice light pair of aluminum shoes?"

"I'd like a pair," said Joan, "only I have to have the kind that comes off at night. My mother makes me take off my shoes when I go to bed."

"Then I can't help you," the blacksmith answered gravely. "When I fit a pair of shoes they stay on, say, between three and four weeks. And now I'd better get my forge going." The forge was electric, and he plugged it into an extension cord that one of the stable boys brought up. Soon the forge began to glow, and the blacksmith called out, "First customer!"

Suzy and Joan had helped to bring in the yearlings earlier so that they would be on hand when the smith was ready for them. They were put into their stalls, and now the girls could see curious heads hanging over the half doors of the stalls, and bright eyes watching for what would happen next. Whickery's head was out, too, but instead of looking around, she was chewing on the wood of the door. She happened to get the knob of the big iron latch in her teeth and, in tugging at it, managed to slide it back.

No one observed that Whickery had done this, and she herself did not know quite what to make of it. As she bent her head for another look at the lock, she pressed against the door which opened at once. Whickery stepped out into the stable yard and was walking quietly around before anyone noticed her.

Suzy, who had wandered back from the truck and usually had an eye out for Whickery, anyway, was the first to notice the open stall door. She called to her father, and he and Ben spun around in the direction of her pointing finger. Whickery was cropping the grass in the far corner of the stable yard, apparently at peace with the world. The men began to walk toward her, talking coaxingly, but Whickery was not interested. She edged out of the corner and started toward the driveway.

"Don't let her get out on the highway!" Mr. Taylor yelled, and Suzy felt almost sick as she thought of the danger. Whickery might easily be hit by a speeding car.

Suzy felt she couldn't bear it if anything happened — it would be like losing a member of the family. And with her would go down the chief hopes of the farm. With her would vanish the prospect of paying the note, maybe even keeping the farm itself. Suzy shuddered and turned quickly to her father, but the little group around the blacksmith's truck had scattered in an attempt to head off Whickery. Whickery knew that she could run faster than any of her pursuers, and loved a game of tag, too. She slipped easily between Mr. Taylor and Ben, who muttered that he heard her laughing as she went by.

Suzy watched despairingly as Whickery trotted down the drive. She knew she could not catch her on foot, so she rushed to the stable and got out Elsinore. Joan followed and the two girls had him bridled in a moment. "I won't waste time with the saddle," panted Suzy, breathless from her hurrying. "Just give me a leg up, Joan."

Joan cupped her hands as she had seen Ben do so often, and with that much assistance Suzy sprang onto Elsinore's bare back. She gathered up the reins, pressed her knees into his sides, and in a moment was trotting down the driveway. She planned to circle around Whickery and come up in front of her. In the excitement of the shoeing she had forgotten to put the usual carrots in her pockets, but Whickery loved clover, and that would probably do for bait.

When Suzy got out on the highway, she looked

around for Whickery. Luckily, that young lady had crossed safely and was heading for the big pasture on the other side. She was cantering along comfortably when she happened to notice Suzy on Elsinore. At once she made as if to turn in the opposite direction, but Elsinore whinnied, and Whickery turned back to see what was going on. Suzy slid off, and with the reins over her arm, started a casual walk toward the runaway. Elsinore, a good teacher like all lead ponies, and used to the whims of horses in training, whinnied once more. Suzy held out her bunch of hastily plucked clover and offered it in a quiet, soothing voice. Whickery looked at Elsinore and Suzy and, yielding to her curiosity, started toward them. The men, who had now reached the pasture, stayed quietly at the edge of the field to see if Suzy's strategy would work. Whickery wavered and started off again, but she was too sociable and curious not to investigate what Elsinore was doing out there. As she came close, she snatched the clover out of Suzy's hand, and Suzy, prepared for this, grabbed her halter. Whickery looked indignant, but Suzy held tight.

"Smart girl, Suzy!" her father called from across the field, and from the relief in his voice, Suzy knew how alarmed he'd been. One of the exercise boys now ran up and caught hold of the halter to lead the runaway back to the stable yard.

"Can't I lead her? I'm the one who caught her."

"You certainly did," her father agreed, "but you haven't a lead rein and you haven't a saddle. Whickery would pull you off Elsinore in no time. Let Sam take her in. And let's all get back and get these babies shod."

Suzy began to sing the lullaby her mother had sung to her when she was tiny:

> Shoe the horses and shoe the mare,
> But let the little colt go bare.

"Daddy, I hate to have Whickery shod."

"You can't keep her a baby by not shoeing her," said Mr. Taylor practically. "Come on, let's get back and see the fun."

By the time Suzy was back in the stable yard, the forge was ruddy with heat, the blacksmith had on his leather apron, and was holding the hoof of one of the yearlings between his knees as he pared it.

"Don't hurt any more than when you cut your toenails," said Ben, with a glance at Suzy's anxious face.

"Aren't the nails going to hurt when he fastens the shoes on?"

"He's an expert; he's not going to hurt. No horse will run if his feet hurt."

Joan, who had followed the chase down to the big pasture, now came up to congratulate Suzy on the capture. It was plain that she felt badly. "You were wonderful, Sue," she said in a small voice. "I wish I could have helped — or caught her myself."

"You did help. I'd never have gotten out there so fast if you hadn't. Let's watch the shoeing now." They went and stood as close to the blacksmith as he would allow.

Whickery was given time to calm down from her prank, and was the last to get her shoes. There had been a good deal of whinnying and restlessness among the yearlings, but as each was shod it was released into a nearby paddock. There, each would run wildly for a bit and then seem to forget the whole matter, and get on with the serious business of grazing.

Suzy stood at Whickery's head, stroking and calming her while the smith worked on her feet. She was glad not to watch, for she couldn't believe it didn't hurt a little. But Whickery was calm, and the two light shoes were soon on — two because she, like most yearlings, had shoes only on her front feet. Young horses turned out together, and playing together, could be injured by a kick from a shod rear hoof. Suzy led off her favorite to the paddock and turned her in. Whickery gave a snort of pleasure at her freedom, and then rushed up and down the length of the field. After that she lay on her side for a minute and then turned over twice in rapid succession. She ended up with all four feet in the air and stayed in that position for a long interval, rocking back and forth.

"She's admiring her new shoes!" Suzy called to Ben.

"She's not studying about shoes — she's scratching her back," said Ben.

Chapter SEVEN

A Saturday or two later, Mr. Taylor said at breakfast, "You want to come out with me, Sue? We're going to put the boys on the yearlings today."

In a few minutes they were on their way to the stables. For the last week the yearlings had spent much of their time in the stalls, first with a blanket, and later with a loosely fastened saddle across their backs. Whickery, high-strung and impatient, had tried to get rid of each the moment it was put on her. After a few days she accepted the blanket, but the saddle was another matter. She walked as close to the walls of her stall as she could get, rubbing against them and trying to scrape the saddle off. When she found after repeated tries that she could not do it, she began to tremble. She would not cease her restless walking. Up and down the short length of the stall she went, up and down, up and down, until Suzy was worried and went to see Ben

about it. He stood watching for a while and tried to soothe her, but Whickery continued her restless pacing.

"Acting like a wild bird in a cage, ain't she?" he said to Suzy, and they went off together to find Mr. Taylor and bring him to the stable.

"Looks to me like Whickery is fixing to be a real stall walker," Ben said to Mr. Taylor. "And I don't like the way she sweats and trembles."

Mr. Taylor watched Whickery a few minutes, talked to Ben, and their decision was made to cut the time she wore the saddle to almost nothing, and slowly work up to the normal period.

Whickery tolerated the saddle a minute or two, and then she would begin again her restless march. Suzy tried staying in the stall with her, petting and comforting her, but Whickery was excited and unfriendly. She laid her ears back and started to rear, and Mr. Taylor made Suzy come out.

"There's another trick we'll try," he said. "We'll get her a friend to distract her." He went off then, and pretty soon came back with Jo-Boy, a spotted, half-grown coach dog.

Horses and dogs are traditionally friends, and Whickery looked at the newcomer with interest. Jo-Boy rushed around the stall, smelling everything and then inquisitively approached Whickery. She seemed to think he came too near, and backed off. Jo-Boy persisted, and in irritation Whickery raised her hind leg to kick him.

Ben sprang to her head to calm her, and Mr. Taylor took Jo-Boy outside.

"That doesn't mean a thing," said Mr. Taylor. "Feed Jo-Boy in the stall and give him plenty so he'll go to sleep afterward. If he's quiet, Whickery will take to him."

"Suppose she doesn't?" Suzy asked.

"Then we'll try a goat or another dog she might like better. But I think she'll like Jo-Boy."

Jo-Boy's bed was made up in a corner of the stall — it was an old sack with clean straw under it — his feeding and water bowls were put there, and even a couple of bones. By the second day Whickery had accepted him, and by the third, they were friends. She seemed to like having company, for her pacing slackened and gradually ceased. When a blanket was strapped on her again, she tried to shake it off but did not fight it as she had before. A few more days, and the saddle was put on over the blanket and left for fifteen minutes. Although Whickery tried as usual to scrape it off, she seemed merely irritated rather than panicky, the way she had been before. Jo-Boy was with her constantly; the stall was his home as well as hers, and they seemed to have a real affection for each other. When he went off on one of his occasional expeditions, Whickery looked around uneasily for him until his return.

After about two weeks, when Whickery had learned to treat the saddle calmly, one of the exercise boys was put up. He did not attempt to sit, but just lay across the saddle so Whickery could get used to the weight of a rider. Suzy watched, then begged to be allowed to do it too, but her father was adamant.

"Whickery is pretty quick. She could send you flying through the air with the greatest of ease. I don't want to be picking you out of the shrubbery."

"Sam does it."

"Sam didn't, when he was your age. No soap, old girl."

Suzy watched enviously, but when Whickery began to buck a little, she was not sorry to be on the firm earth. As Whickery's feet left the ground, Sam slid out of the saddle and hit the ground with a thud.

"I know how to fall," he boasted, up on his feet in a second, and darting out of the way of Whickery's heels.

"Think she's getting too many oats, Ben?" Mr. Taylor asked. "She's so frisky."

"She needs every one. She's going to be powerful when she's full grown. I look for her to bring in more trophies than you and Mrs. Taylor got room for."

Mr. Taylor laughed, but Suzy was sure that Ben was right.

"But about oats —" Ben started after Mr. Taylor. "Somebody else is getting too many, not Whickery. They keep on disappearing, and we keep on not catching the thief."

"You still haven't a clue as to who's taking them?"

"I thought I had. I had it boiled down to where it had to be one of four men, but every one of them was able to account for himself the night the last oats disappeared. They even had witnesses. I had to start figuring all over again, and I can't seem to come up with an answer."

"It's the anxiety as well as the loss we can't afford," said Mr. Taylor. "Makes me wonder what'll disappear next. You'd think with dogs and a watchman, and all of us on the lookout — " He gave a worried shrug.

"I still think it's got to be somebody who knows the place well. But you can't accuse a man of being a thief just because you think it's likely."

"No. No, you can't. But this is certainly the time when every leak ought to be plugged. The feed-store bill last month was something to curl my hair." Mr. Taylor stroked his straight dark hair thoughtfully.

Suzy had been listening quietly, and now said, "I have an idea. Could I — "

"No, you couldn't," said her father, without waiting for her to finish. "And get any ideas you've got out of your head at once. This is men's work — leave it to the men. It's only in comic books that children are successful detectives."

"Yes, sir," said Suzy. She didn't dare argue anything when her father was in this mood, but she thought rudely that if it were men's work it was too bad the men didn't get on with it.

At school the next day, she told Joan the idea her father had been too impatient to listen to.

"I think it's swell," said Joan, "but do you know enough?"

"Not yet, I don't, but I can join the school camera club and —"

"I'll join, too! Only thing is, I haven't a camera."

"I have two. You can use my old Brownie, and I'll use the one I got for my birthday. And we won't tell a soul why we're so interested." Both girls solemnly crossed their hearts and then hooked little fingers as a further pledge of secrecy.

Meantime, the serious business of training Whickery had really begun. The stall training had lasted two weeks, and at the end of that time Whickery did not seem to notice the saddle any more than she did the halter which she had worn since she was a tiny foal. The next big step was to get her used to the bridle. Ben slipped it on her so quickly and deftly that at first she didn't seem to know what had happened. Then she tried to spit the bridle out. Of course it wouldn't come out, so she turned her head and looked inquiringly at Ben who was standing beside her, petting her.

"It's all right," he assured her, gently scratching the handsome bay neck. "I don't say you're going to like it, but I do say you'll get used to it —"

Whickery lifted her head and stared, and Suzy, who was on hand to help with the chores, cried, "Ben, she doesn't believe you. She understands every word you say and she knows you're — "

"I'm for sure not kidding," said Ben. "She will be used to that bridle in two-three days. If she don't have it on, she'll act like a lady that's forgotten her handkerchief or something when she's going to a party. That true, Whick?" he added, turning back to Whickery, who began to smell him all over as if he were something new she had to learn about.

As Ben predicted, the yearlings quickly became used to the bridles and were not bothered by them. The next step was for the exercise boys to sit in the saddles. Their feet hung loosely out of the stirrups until the trainees were used to the new position. Everything was done gradually so as to keep the horses from being frightened or nervous.

Whickery did not like these new things and began stall-walking again. Her training periods were again cut down and she was given extra care and attention, but her restless pacing continued. Ben came into her stall one day, leading a young goat. Whickery stood still to watch as the goat ran around sniffing everything. Jo-Boy joined in the sniffing game, and soon the two were romping together. Whickery continued to watch and occasionally gave them a little nip, or threatened them with a lifted hoof when they came too close.

Suzy thought the goat took a good deal of punishment from the other two, but Ben said, "Let him learn his place. If Whickery is too hard on him, he'll soon be big enough to butt her right back."

Suzy laughed at the idea of the goat being so bold, but Ben said he had seen it happen with other horses. One day Suzy herself saw it happen. The goat, who was of course named Billy, was frisking around the stall, and tried to pull a bit of hay that Whickery was chewing right out of her mouth. Whickery was so startled that for a moment she did nothing, but then she dropped the hay and gave Billy a sharp nip. He ran to the corner of the stall, turned round with lowered head, and started for Whickery.

"Hey, none of that!" Ben called. As usual, he was nearby and had heard Suzy's cries of excitement. He led Billy out of the stall and tied him up for a while.

"It's just as much Whickery's fault," said Suzy, who liked things to be fair.

"Miss Whickery," said Ben, "is going to be one of the best race horses in the country, and we've got to take care of her and not let her get hurt, even when it's her own fault. Mr. Billy is just common ordinary goat and able — too able — to watch out for himself. He'll lose his stable job if he tries any butting."

Suzy understood better what Ben meant when a few days later Whickery hurt herself. Just because she felt frisky, Whickery was racing around the paddock, and misjudged the distance before she could stop. She crashed into the fence and went limping off. Dr. Plumm was summoned, looked grave, and finally bandaged her

hock. Whickery hated this, though the doctor said it didn't hurt. Immediately he had finished, she began to tear at the bandage with her strong white teeth.

"Bring the cradle, Ben," the doctor called, and before Whickery could protest, the cradle was slipped over her neck. The cradle was made of light but strong aluminum, and while Whickery could move her head around, she couldn't stretch far enough over it to reach the injured hock.

Suzy had been watching the doctor and now ran back to the house and got her camera.

"What you want a picture of that for?" Ben asked. "Take her when she looks pretty. That cradle's no ornament."

"I just like to take pictures."

"You sure do. Every which way I turn, I hear that shutter clicking. How come you got so fond of it?"

"I just did. There's a camera club at school, you know."

"I bet they're mighty tired of horse pictures."

"I'll have something different before long," said Suzy, looking smug. "I'm learning about flash pictures now, so I can take some night things. Maybe I'll get a weasel or a fox."

Ben laughed heartily. "I'd just like to see you get close enough to either one to snap his picture."

"I'll fool you yet, Ben!" Suzy picked up a bucket of feed and started on the evening round.

Whickery spent her convalescence mostly alone in her stall or in a small paddock. She fretted at her confinement, but Ben was firm. "Turn her out with the other fillies, she'd get to skylarking sure," he said when Suzy tried to get extra privileges for her favorite.

"But she's so lonesome." Suzy had put her feed bucket down and stood in the stall scratching Whickery's nose.

"She's missed the others something scandalous," Ben agreed. "If she hadn't had Jo-Boy and Billy to talk to, I don't know what she would have done. But of course they're not as good company as her own kind."

"Talk, did they!" said Suzy scornfully. "Talk! Stop trying to fool me. What language did they talk?"

"Animal. You may not understand them, but they understand each other." And he walked off in a dignified way that ended the conversation.

Whickery was lucky; the injured place healed rapidly, and in a few days she was able to go back to her training with the other yearlings. They were now well along, accustomed to saddle and bridle, and to a rider with his feet in the stirrups. Early each morning they went out to the exercise ring to walk, trot, and canter. After two months of this, Mr. Taylor told Suzy they were ready for their first try on the real training track. "Want to get up early and see?" he asked.

Suzy nodded. "And may Joan come?"

It was Friday, so Joan came to spend the night, and the girls promised not to talk late, as they had to be up at five, but there were enough giggles for Mrs. Taylor to rap on the door and call for quiet. Suzy and Joan eyed each other. They were bursting with conversation, but they *had* promised. Suzy hopped out of bed and went to the medicine chest and returned with her mouth neatly taped with adhesive. This made it impossible for her to speak, so she merely looked at Joan and held out the adhesive and scissors. Joan cut off a length and fitted it over her mouth, though giggling made this difficult.

Suzy wrote on a pad, "I wish I could get a picture of us."

Joan seized the pencil and started to reply, but Mrs. Taylor's step was heard in the hall, so both girls dived into bed and snapped out the lights. Unable to see each other and unable to talk, they were soon asleep.

In the morning, they pulled off what was left of each other's adhesive, squealing as they did so because the adhesive clung and hurt as it was pulled away from the skin. With that done, the giggles at each other's appearance stopped and the girls dressed quickly. They were downstairs in the hall, waiting, when Mr. Taylor appeared.

"Good morning, early birds," he said. "Into the car with you." They drove the half mile to the track, taking the short cut across the fields. The early morning air seemed to have a special freshness, and Suzy and Joan took long breaths of it.

"What's that poem we had in English the other day?" Suzy asked. "You know: ' — the long light shakes across the lakes, — ' That's the way the sunshine looks. Only there aren't any lakes, but this much dew makes the grass look like green water."

Mr. Taylor had driven across the track and into the long oval in its middle. He stopped the car near a raised, covered platform. This commanded a view of the whole track, and Mr. Taylor at once started to climb the steep steps that led to it. The trainer, already there, waved to them, but instead of climbing up, too, the girls raced to the stable to watch the saddling up. The lead pony had already been saddled, and was standing quietly at the rack. Some of the yearlings were led out to stand beside him while their saddles and bridles were put on. His calm presence seemed to soothe them, and their twitchiness subsided. When Whickery was led out to be saddled, she put on her own little show, tossing her head to avoid the bridle, and fidgeting so that it was almost impossible to tighten the saddle girth.

"Bring Jo-Boy out," said Ben, and one of the stable boys ran to get him. Jo-Boy came on a leash, which he seemed to regard as an indignity, but Ben would take no chances of his getting on the track. With Jo-Boy and the lead pony near, and Suzy at her head soothing her, Whickery calmed down.

"She's all right now," Ben said. "You better run for the platform. We're going to start the first three in a minute." The girls ran back and climbed to the platform where Mr. Taylor and the trainer stood.

"Now we'll see how well these babies have learned what we're trying to teach them," said Mr. Taylor, as the first group appeared on the track and followed the lead pony to the starting gate.

Just as at a real race course, the gate spanning the track was divided into compartments. At a signal, a mechanism would open the barrier in front of each horse so that he would be free to run. The lead pony walked confidently into his compartment and the others followed, though warily, with some tossing of heads and every now and then a whinny of protest. Heads still tossed but at last each horse stood ready in its own compartment, the barriers pulled back, and they were off.

For the last week they had done their walking, trotting, and cantering. This morning they were to do their first running. It is called breezing. As the gate lifted, the lead pony, Sir Knight, started off at a run and, as usual, the others followed him. Sir Knight quickly fell back. The others rushed on. For the first few times the trainer would permit them to run only short distances — first, an eighth of a mile, then a quarter, then longer, as their muscles hardened and toned up.

The first set of three ran and then started back for the stable. Then the next set came up. Whickery was in the final set, and Suzy felt she could hardly wait to see Whickery actually running on a track. "Dad, may I hold the stop watch?" she asked, and her father nodded.

"They're off!" he called as the gate opened. Suzy pressed down the button on the stop watch. Only seconds later, she pressed the button again. The yearlings had run their limit, and the exercise boys reined them in to avoid their getting too tired or winded on their first runs. Suzy thought there had never been a prettier sight than Whickery flying down the track. She turned to her father who was smiling broadly. "Did Whickery do all right?" she asked, holding up the stop watch.

"I'll say she did. Looks to me as if she were going to have Falada's speed; now, if she's just inherited her sire's stamina — " He looked reflective, for only time would reveal that.

The yearlings were sweating freely after their run, and Suzy and Joan walked down to watch them being cooled off. Whickery was standing, while a groom sponged her. Alcohol had been added to the water for its bracing effect, and though the water itself was warm, Whickery shivered as the sponge went over her flanks, wiping away the sweaty dust. Next, a scraper was run rapidly over her whole body, and the extra water dripped off. Finally a sheet was thrown over her, and Joan stared in surprise. "I guess they'll put a bathrobe on her next," she said.

Suzy was a little offended. "They've got to be careful not to let her catch cold or let her muscles stiffen. Now look. They're not through."

The groom had attached a lead rein to Whickery's halter and was leading her around in a large circle. A bucket of water with a little bran in it was placed at one side, and every time Whickery passed it, she was allowed to take a quick sip. This made her rather indignant. She was thirsty after her run and would have liked to empty the bucket in one long, delicious draft. But she ought not to chill her stomach with so much cold water at one time, so as soon as she had had her sip, the groom pulled her up again. She continued her walk for forty-five minutes until she was normally cool again, and by that time the bucket was empty.

The girls stood watching for a few minutes as the procession of yearlings walked around the circle, and then Mr. Taylor came up and said, "I heard rumors there'd be batter cakes for breakfast. Let's get back before Mother is really mad with us for being late."

Joan gestured at the sheeted, walking horses. "When will they get breakfast?"

"When they're thoroughly cooled down. And they'll get something they like as much as I like batter cakes."

The car drove off across the grass of the pasture, heading for the road and the big house.

Chapter EIGHT

BREAKFAST OVER, Suzy and Joan wandered around for a while. After their early start on the day, it seemed much later than it actually was, and each girl was inclined to be a little cross and to want her own way.

Finally Suzy said, "We might have a rehearsal."

"Rehearse *what?*"

"You know: my — I mean our — plan."

"They'll never let you out at night so that you can work it," said Joan, deflatingly.

"I won't ask. But I'm going to ask Mother now for some money to buy flash bulbs. They ought not to have to come out of my teeny-weeny allowance."

Suzy was back in a few minutes. "She says all right, and if Ben says we can take the lead ponies, we can saddle up and ride over to the store and get them."

Ben agreed, and it was not long before the girls were trotting along the sandy side of the road toward the store, three miles away. After lunch on return, Suzy and

Joan went down to the stables.

"We'll creep in," said Suzy, "so Ben won't see us." But they were hardly in the room where the oats were stored before Ben stuck his head in.

"What you doing in here? It's not near time to feed."

"I'm practicing taking flashlight pictures."

"You know the rules about fires and matches."

"This is an *electric* flash. I wouldn't so much as have a match in my pocket when I come to the stables. You know that. Just show me where I can plug in, and let me have an extension cord. Please, Ben."

"Well, all right," said Ben unwillingly. "I got a feeling you're up to something, but I don't know what."

"You've heard about our camera club?"

"Too much," said Ben, going off for the extension cord.

Suzy and Joan spent an hour or so in the oat room, busy with the extension cord and some string. But at feeding time they were both on hand to help.

"I didn't see any flash," said Ben.

"Sometime you will. This was practice." Suzy winked at Joan.

Never before had Suzy paid such close attention to the training, but now her mother said she almost had to use a lead rein to get her daughter from the stables. Indeed, Suzy would have liked to be up at five every morning to see the horses breezed. Breezing was fun to watch, and the horses, too, seemed to enjoy it. As their muscles hardened and their speed increased, they finally worked up to a real run. The trainer was there with his stop watch to see how fast they went, and the breezing had some of the excitement of a race. It seemed very hard to Suzy that her mother would not allow her to be on hand.

"Be reasonable, Sue. You'd be tired by the time school begins and asleep in the afternoons. Learning is your job now, just as it is Whickery's. Only you're learning different things."

"I wish Whickery could have my share of French, and I'd do her lining up at the gate — she hates it, Mother — and backing up after the race is over. I wouldn't mind going in the gate — and she does."

"Speak to your teacher," said Mrs. Taylor, laughing. "If she'll take Whickery in her class, I'll agree to the other part."

Suzy walked off. Why did grown people always think they were so *funny?* After a minute, she headed for the paddock where the mares and foals were grazing. Falada had had a colt in the spring, and though Suzy loved him, she was a little jealous of him for Whickery's sake. As he trotted up to the fence beside his mother, she merely patted him and gave one carrot to Falada. The other was for Whickery, and the colt was not going to tease it away from her. As Suzy sat on the fence, still cross with her mother, she glanced down — and there on the ground lay another match! No oats had been stolen in the last ten days, but *somebody* had been around. What could he be up to? Only an intruder would strike a match. Perhaps, as Daddy had said might happen, the thief was getting bolder and eying other things?

Suzy resolved to put her plan into execution that very night. She had meant to, several times, but it was hard to stay awake until her parents were asleep and she could safely slip out of the house. But tonight she would, and she wouldn't take the chance of napping first. She could make no preparations while people were still around, so she might as well not think about them until after supper. Now she decided to get her bicycle and ride to the stable near the track where Whickery and the other horses in training now stayed. The new crop of foals, weanlings, and yearlings occupied the stables near the house where Whickery and her friends used to be.

Even though the path to the stable was sandy, it was quicker to ride than to walk it. Once there, she leaned her bike against the big oak and went over to the small paddock where Whickery was standing. Suzy began to talk softly, and Whickery came over at once and ran her soft nose over Suzy's jacket until she located the carrot, and then pulled it out of the concealing pocket. This was a game both girl and filly loved, and when the carrot was gone, Suzy let Whickery take the apple she her-

self was eating. "How're you coming, Whickery?" she asked. "Please save your fastest run for Saturday when Joan and I can watch!"

Whickery made no answer, but Mr. Taylor saw his daughter at the fence and came over.

"Good news, Suzy," he said, pulling a letter out of his pocket. "The Jockey Club has passed *Whickery* as a name, so now it's official."

"Oh, Dad! The name I thought of myself! I guess it must be a pretty good one!"

"Any name is good if the horse is a winner. And that's what I think your friend Whickery is going to be."

"Daddy, when will she have her first race?"

"In the spring. We'll stop training in another ten days and turn them out. Then we'll pick them up again after New Year's and really put them through a course of sprouts. Then off to the tracks, and we'll find out just how good they are."

Suzy stored all this up to tell Joan next day, but she had another question. She asked almost timidly, "Will they wait that long on the bank loan?"

Mr. Taylor frowned. "Yes and no. They've been pressing me, but I've been able to pay a little, though not as much as the bank would like. However, they know as well as I do, there's no sense in pushing me too hard. What I think they have in mind is to see how well we do in the spring racing season. If we have another bad year, I don't think they'll be very patient."

"Whickery will be running in the spring."

"She certainly will. I expect great things of her. Don't worry, Sue. We'll all do our job the best we know how, and I think things will work out."

With that, Suzy had to be content, but it made her more determined than ever to catch the thief. That would save money for Daddy and maybe help pacify the bank. For the next two or three nights she kept herself awake until her parents had gone to bed. Then she slipped out of bed — it was scary in the dark! — and crept down the stairs and out of the house. She went to the oat room and set up her camera. The string across the door, which was to trap any intruder, would also set off the flash bulb and release the camera shutter, and she would have a picture of the thief. Nothing happened the first two nights, but as Suzy went sleepily out the third morning to hide her equipment until night, she saw an indignant Ben sprawled flat among the oats.

"You stretch that string across the door?" he asked angrily.

Suzy nodded.

"It tripped me, and I fell flat and like to broke my neck. And that flash bulb scared me out of ten years' growth!"

"Then the trap worked!" cried Suzy exultantly. "But I'm sorry I caught you, Ben."

"You better be," said Ben, rubbing his neck vigorously. "I'm not the age when falling's a pleasure. What're you up to, anyway?"

Suzy explained her carefully worked out plan. "And when the real thief comes along and stumbles over the string, we'll have his picture, and then we can catch him. But please don't tell Daddy."

"That's a real smart plan," said Ben, still rubbing his neck. "We won't say a word to your papa until it works. You show me how and I'll set the camera, and you go to sleep. You look mighty peaky."

"I'm just terribly sleepy," said Suzy, trying to stifle a huge yawn. "We'll be partners, Ben, but don't tell a soul."

"Not me. And when you get that picture of me falling on my face, you give it to me. I don't want anybody to see it."

"All right," said Suzy, grinning. "You did look funny." She ran back to the house to dress for breakfast.

At school that morning, Suzy was in a fever of impatience for recess to come, so that she could tell Joan about trapping Ben.

"Was he hurt much?" Joan asked, torn between concern and amusement.

"More mad than hurt. I think it's pretty good to have him for a partner, don't you? I'm so sleepy I could die."

"I guess so. But it would have been grand to do it all yourself."

That was what Suzy thought too, so she changed the subject hastily. "I forgot to tell you: Daddy says we're going to stop training soon and turn the horses out until after Christmas."

"I should think in three months they'd forget everything if they stop training."

"You don't forget everything you know because school doesn't keep all year. Horses would go stale if they trained all the time. They need vacations, too."

Joan would have liked to argue this, but when Suzy was in one of her *moods* about the rights of horses, it was no use saying anything.

Chapter NINE

TRAINING CEASED, and Suzy thought things were rather dull around the farm without it. But one night the quiet was splintered by a cry so chilling that Suzy sat straight up in bed, wide awake. What *could* it be? Half a dozen ideas flashed through her mind. A wolf? A neighboring farmer swore he'd seen a gray wolf recently on the edge of the woods, but Daddy said that was nonsense; there hadn't been a wolf in the county in a hundred years. It wasn't a fox. A fox barked like a dog, and no dog could make such a deep, frightening howl. Just then the cry came again, but weaker, and followed by what seemed a jumble of words. They *were* words: now she could hear plainly, "Lord help me! Lord help me!"

A frightened Suzy started to slide under the covers, when she heard a familiar step in the hall. She ran to her door and opened it, just in time to see her father disappearing down the stairs, a robe over his pajamas and a pistol in his hand. If he was going somewhere, Suzy wanted to go too. There was no time to ask — she heard the front door slam as he left the house — and besides he might say no. "But he hasn't said it," Suzy argued with herself, and started to hurry into her clothes. She'd just creep out, and so quietly Mother wouldn't hear or stop her and try to get an idea of what was going on. The howls and the frightened voice had stopped, but there were different voices now, all talking in loud, excited tones.

In another moment, Suzy was on the stairs, and when she opened the front door, she was surprised to find all the lights on in the nearby stables. She could see her father and the watchman standing at the door of the oats room — and Ben, who slept nearby, running up to join them. Slipping from bush to bush, and careful to stay in the shadows, Suzy crept closer. As she peered between the men she saw another man, tripped as Ben had been tripped, sitting on a pile of oats and looking bewildered and afraid.

"I came in here," he was saying, "just to get me some oats for my mules. I got a heavy hauling job tomorrow, and those mules need the oats. I stepped in the door and there was a big flash — like to blinded me — and there I was face down in the oats."

"You can't have stayed face down long," said Ben. "When I heard you, you were yelling fit to raise the dead."

"Course I yelled. I never was so scared in all my born

days. I thought my time had come. A big, bright light like that coming from nowhere, it's naturally obliged to be lightning. I ain't positive yet I'm not struck." The man started to feel his body and to move his arms and legs, to be sure they were all right.

"You haven't been struck by lightning," said Mr. Taylor sharply, "but the law's about to get you. That's going to be your trouble, Sully, not lightning."

Suzy gave a start when her father said "Sully." Sully was the stableman fired for laziness when they were first beginning to cut down running expenses on the farm. Of course he would know his way around, know the dogs, know the night watchman's routine progress, and all 'the good hiding places which would avoid him. He was one of the four men Ben had been sure of. He must have been as wily as a weasel to fool Ben, who had been so close to catching him.

Ben was looking at Sully now, anger and dislike in his face. "You're worthless," he said to Sully, "just plain worthless. It ain't just oats you been stealing, but other folks' time and work and peace. I hope now you're tangled up with the law they don't just keep you in some nice, comfortable jail. You need to do some work, hard work, to teach you a lesson. Like working in a road gang, breaking rocks maybe."

"Lock him up, Ben," Mr. Taylor interrupted, "and I'll phone the sheriff. By the way, what *was* the flash he saw?"

"That was my trap," said Suzy, coming out of the

shadows, and unable to keep quiet any longer. "*Now* don't you think it was a good idea?"

"I'm not sure what you mean. What idea? What trap?"

"I tried to tell you when I thought of it, but you wouldn't listen. My nature magazine always has pictures of wild animals, pictures they take themselves. There's a string or something, and the animals walk into it getting to the bait, and that sets off a flash bulb — and the picture's taken. So I thought we could do the same thing in the oat room. But you just talked about comic-book detectives."

"I did at that," Mr. Taylor admitted, remembering. "I apologize, dear. I'm dumb, but I'm glad I've got a smart daughter." He bent down and kissed her. "Catching the thief is going to make the difference of a good many hundreds of dollars. I won't get the cold shivers when the feed-store bill comes in." He laughed. "Some months I could hardly make myself open it. That's over, thanks to you."

"Oh, Dad!" Suzy said, and stopped. Her father's praise was very sweet, but she didn't want to sound vain by agreeing with it. She wasn't going to deny it, either; after all, she *was* the one responsible for catching Sully. Her thoughts were interrupted by the arrival of the farm dogs, who rushed up to Sully and jumped on him affectionately.

"How do you like that!" exclaimed Mr. Taylor.

"Those dogs ought to go to jail along with Sully."

"Will Sully have to go to jail?" Suzy asked in a low voice. She and her father had started walking toward the house, and she turned a worried face to him now.

"Of course he'll have to. Don't waste any sympathy on *him*. He had a good job here, and he was too lazy to keep it. He wouldn't work for me and he won't work for himself, or just enough to get by. I drove by his house the other day. The front porch had fallen in, and instead of repairing it, he was sitting with his back against it, asleep. He's taken bushels and bushels of oats, a lot more than would feed any mules he owns. Probably sold what he didn't need. He's *trifling*, that's what he is, and this getting caught will do him a world of good. Come on, young lady, let's get to bed. It's barely four o'clock."

As they walked into the hall, they saw Mrs. Taylor. Her expression changed from anxiety to surprise as she saw Suzy. "Suzy!" she exclaimed. "I thought you were in your bed, fast asleep. What — ?"

"Don't scold her," said Mr. Taylor. "It seems the men on the place couldn't do it, but a certain red-haired young lady, with a bright idea we wouldn't even listen to, has trapped the thief."

"What *are* you talking about?"

Mr. Taylor obligingly repeated what had happened, and Suzy felt almost embarrassed at the lavish praise of both her parents. "Mother, do I have to go back to bed?"

she asked by way of changing the subject. "I'd never go to sleep again."

"While Dad phones the sheriff, we'll go in the kitchen and have some hot cocoa," her mother suggested, "and after that maybe bed will seem a more reasonable idea."

They sat around the table, hashing over the events of the night, and before Suzy knew it, she began to nod. Her father looked over at her and smiled. "Let's go up before I have to carry you. It wouldn't be suitable for the stupid owner to carry the lady detective who saved the old home place."

Bed felt delicious, and just as Suzy was thinking of all she'd have to tell Joan next morning, she fell asleep. It seemed not five minutes later that her mother was shaking her and saying, "It's late, dear. After seven. Wake up, Sherlock Holmes."

Suzy hurried through her breakfast so as to have time to run and have a word with Ben before going to school. There was one question she had to ask him: "You were the one who suspected Sully all along. How did he fool you and get away?"

Ben looked sheepish. "You mean the time we found that cigarette box? I went after those four men, and every one of them could tell where he was that night, and had folks to swear to it. And I believed them."

"Sully, too?"

"Sully. I got the real story out of him while we were waiting for the sheriff. Seems he took his wife and children and went over to spend two-three days with his mother-in-law in Boulton. Things was kind of crowded, and Sully had to sleep on the porch. He didn't sleep so good. He said it made him mad to hear the rest of them snoring. After a while he got up and took his car out. He said the first thing he knew, he was turning into the back road here at Cherrydale."

"We're twenty miles from Boulton," Suzy snorted. "I suppose that car drove itself."

Ben smiled. "This is Sully's tale, not mine. He said he stopped the car, and when the dogs came rushing up, he just took them in the car with him. Seems he just accidentally had a couple of nice bones along."

"Accidentally!"

"He says. He and the dogs waited until the watchman passed. Then he took what he wanted and was back in Boulton asleep at breakfast time, and the rest of the folks had to wake him. They never knew he'd been anywhere. At the time, he told me he was in Boulton that night. I checked with his family and the neighbors, and they all said the same thing. I believed them. He sure outsmarted me." Ben rubbed his forehead.

"That's not your fault," said Suzy indignantly. "You've got honest brains — and how would you know what some old thief would think up?"

Ben looked pleased. "That's mighty nice. But I wish I'd shined up my brains to be brighter than his." He cocked an ear. "That your bus I hear coming?"

"It is!"

Suzy picked up her books and flew down the driveway.

Time was passing. Christmas came and went, and after that a spell of cold weather set in. It snowed, and rained, and then snowed again, and Suzy began to worry about the training. The horses, too, were restless, as Ben would not leave them out overnight in 'falling' weather, and they hated being confined. There was a good deal of neighing from the stables, disconsolate heads hung out over the half doors of stalls, and from the young stallions' quarters came a noise that sounded like hammering, but was actually only impatient hoofs kicking against the side walls.

Mr. Taylor, making the rounds with Ben, said, "I think we'll start them on the covered track. They won't get a run there but they can work off some energy and start to get into condition."

The covered track was not far from the big one. It, too, was an oval, though a much smaller one. It was roofed and partly boarded on the outside, "to keep out," Mr. Taylor smilingly told Suzy, "the coarsest of the rain and snow." It was protected enough anyhow to keep the sandy track fairly dry, and that meant less danger of the horses' slipping and wrenching — or perhaps breaking — a leg.

The horses came out in the usual groups of three, and

seemed glad to start their training again, especially as the hated gate was too wide to be used on the smaller, covered track. Whickery trembled a little as the tack was put on her after her vacation from it, but Jo-Boy and Billy were near, and the lead pony was brought close enough for her to see him. This reassured her, and she relaxed and let Ben tighten the saddle girth without any more fuss.

For the first few days the horses walked, trotted, and cantered around the covered track as they had at the beginning of their training. This was to leg them up, as the trainer called it, but Suzy understood better when Ben said, "They lost some of their muscles and wind while they were turned out. This is the way they get it back."

At the end of ten days the weather, though still cold, had cleared considerably, and the horses went back to the big track. Now they really ran. Suzy, watching, thought it was the prettiest sight in the world.

The days drifted into spring. The horses had trained for nearly three months, and Mr. Taylor said rather grimly that the time for the test had come.

Joan, who as usual was spending Saturday with Suzy, said anxiously, "Mr. Taylor, why does Whickery have to race? Suppose she doesn't like it?"

"She'll like it. That's what her whole training has been, to get her ready for racing. Racing is like an examination. It shows how good the horses are at what they've learned. We think Whickery is pretty speedy. But other breeders and trainers aren't going to take my word for it. They've got some pretty speedy fillies, too, that they think as much of as you and Suzy and I think of Whickery. These girls have to prove themselves on the tracks, and then there's no argument."

"Will Whickery go right in the Derby?" Joan asked, and Suzy was embarrassed. How could Joan be so dumb, she thought.

"You don't go into college from kindergarten," she said coldly, before her father could answer.

"Maybe she'll never be good enough," said Mr. Taylor, ignoring Suzy and answering Joan. "Only the very best horses are entered for it. The sure way to find out which *are* the best horses is to put them in other races and see how well they do. Whickery will start off as a two-year-old, running against other two-year-old fillies. If she does as well as Sue and I think she's going to, she *will* be entered for the Derby when she's a three-year-old. Though very few fillies have won it."

"Aren't fillies as good as colts?" Joan asked jealously.

"Some of them are. But a colt is usually bigger and stronger than a filly, just as boys are usually bigger and stronger than girls. The Derby takes staying powers as well as speed — it's a mile and a quarter course — and while we know Whickery has speed, we don't know how much stamina she's got. If we knew all the answers we wouldn't have to race," he added smiling, and went off with Ben to have a look at the yearlings.

"I just said 'the Derby.' I don't know what it really is," Joan admitted as the men walked away.

"It's a race they have in Kentucky every year. There are lots of big races, but Daddy says the Derby is the most famous of them all. If your horse wins *that*, well —" Suzy's eyes grew dreamy, and she saw almost as clearly as if it were happening, Whickery — tearing down the Derby track — all the other horses far behind her — !

"Wake up, Sue, I know now." Joan gave her an impatient little shake, and Suzy returned from her brief Kentucky visit, to the farm, to Joan, to Saturday afternoon, and to a ride on the lead ponies.

The next Friday when Suzy and Joan came home from school, the big horse van was drawn up in the stable yard, and was being washed and polished. Suzy rushed over to Ben who was supervising.

"Starting for New York and the tracks tomorrow early," said Ben, before Suzy could get a word out.

"Ben, may we look around inside?"

Ben gave them a hand up, and the two girls walked the length of the van. "It's as big as a house trailer!" Joan exclaimed in awe.

"Six stalls. I guess it is."

They examined the stalls, three at each end of the truck, and took an experimental lie-down on the clean straw which covered the floor. There was provision, too, for the horses' feed and water, and two cots for the men who would sleep inside.

"Who's going, Ben?" Suzy asked, reappearing at the door of the van.

"Whickery, four of her friends, a lead pony, Jo-Boy, and Billy. I don't suppose you're interested in the humans," Ben added with a grin. The girls looked embarrassed, but Ben was right.

"Are you going to see the race?" Joan asked wistfully, but Suzy shook her head.

"You have to be sixteen to be allowed at the tracks. It's a law."

"Scoot now," said Ben, appearing at the door and holding out his hands, but the girls ignored him and jumped from the big center door of the van.

The next morning they were up in time to see the ramp put up to the center door, and the horses who were to go, led up to it.

The horses looked at the ramp suspiciously because it was new to them, but Sir Knight, the lead pony, had traveled in vans before, and walked up the ramp confidently. He turned and looked at his companions as if to reassure them, but they were pulling against their lead reins and whinnying. Finally, Ben brought Sir Knight out again, and with the pony directly in front, tried to lead his little procession in.

Four followed but Whickery still balked until Billy,

who smelled fresh hay, took one jump and ran nimbly up the ramp. Then Whickery stopped pulling against her rein and walked up the ramp herself, escorted by Jo-Boy, with only a few tossings of her pretty head.

The stable boys with their suitcases were last up the ramp. Then it was pulled in like a ship's gangplank. The big center doors were shut. The driver gunned the motor, and the big van started slowly down the drive. Everyone watched as it went off. It seemed rather a solemn moment, and Ben said, "There's a lot of hopes going up the road in that van!"

A long series of whinnies came from the truck, and the watchers laughed.

"They're answering you, Ben, and saying, 'Don't worry!'" said Suzy.

Chapter TEN

Suzy waited impatiently for the day Whickery was to run her first race. The van had been gone two weeks, and still Mr. Taylor refused to set a day. He and his trainer talked daily by telephone, and he gave Suzy brief accounts of the conversations. First, the horses were tired from the trip; then one of them got a cold. Everyone worried at this news, for horses find colds as contagious as humans do, and no horse can run his best with his long nose stopped up. The cold cleared up, and eventually the trainer was able to telephone that the horses were in top form, and were just waiting for the word to go.

"You've got it!" said Mr. Taylor, "and I'll come up to see how they make out."

Suzy could think of nothing but the race — and the fact that she couldn't see it. "How old must I be to be allowed to go to the tracks?" she asked, and when Mr. Taylor said, "Sixteen, in New York," she looked delighted.

"That's easy! Everyone says I'm tall for my age, and if Mother will just lend me some of her clothes —"

"My daughter is not going to be a lawbreaker," said her father firmly, "and I'm not going to connive at it. You'll read about the race in the papers, and I'll tell you, and now, Sue, that's the end of it."

Suzy thought she just couldn't bear not to see Whickery's first race, and in spite of her father's prohibition, she edged around the subject a dozen times. The idea she was fondest of was to have her curly red hair cut very short and then to go up as a stable boy. "Nobody could mind that," she argued, "and I know enough about horses to do the work."

"You do," said her father irritably, "but you don't seem to know much about honor. If you're in a game, you play according to the rules, and you don't cheat by changing those rules on the sly. If I connived at it, I'd be in real trouble with the racing association. You aren't the only underage youngster who'd love to go."

At this, Suzy ran up to her room, locked the door, and threw herself across the bed. Her father was just plain cruel! Well, maybe not her father. But the racing officials were! Why couldn't they understand that seeing the race was so terribly important? Especially when you'd helped to bring up the foal yourself, nursed it, looked after it, and done practically everything? She'd ask to go only just this once, and surely the rules could be stretched that much? After all, she was almost fourteen. It wasn't fair!

Suzy sat up. That wasn't true. She'd want to go every single time Whickery raced, of course. Hearing about a race wasn't a nineteenth as good as seeing it. No one would think to tell her the details, such as how Whickery looked when she first came out on the track. Did she lay her ears back when she came to the starting gate, as she often did at the training track, or did she just not notice? Did the announcer's voice booming over the loudspeaker worry her? Oh — there would be a thousand things she would notice if she herself were there, things other people wouldn't think important or worth telling about. Tears pressed against her eyelids, but she was determined to hold them back. She might not be grown up enough to go to the races, but she was grown up enough not to cry. After a while, she got up and walked to the window and stared toward the stables. "What can't be cured must be endured." Ben was always saying that, but the enduring was hard work!

When the day of the race came, Suzy and Joan plastered themselves to the radio to listen, but there was no description of the race and only a brief account of the results. Whickery's name was not mentioned. It just wasn't possible. They had been so sure that all Whickery had to do was to set one dainty foot on the track, and then — she would sweep by all the others as if they weren't there!

Later, Mr. Taylor called up and spoke to Suzy. "Remember, this was Whickery's maiden race," he said. "She isn't used to the crowds and the noise. Once she got started, she ran very well. She'll be buying her own oats pretty soon."

"What does that mean?" Joan asked when Suzy repeated it to her.

"It's sort of like these television contests. There's a prize — a 'purse' it's called — and if your horse comes in first, second, third, or fourth the owner wins some money. Daddy said a horse he used to have, Charming Prince, won two hundred fifty thousand dollars in the years he raced. I was too little to notice, then."

"You must be rich!" said Joan, staring at Suzy.

"We're not. It costs a lot of money to buy all the oats and hay, and pay the stablemen and trainer — and — oh, everything. Dad says if he can make a normal business profit he thinks he's lucky. And besides — " Suzy started to speak of the loan that now hung threateningly over everything, but she knew her father would be furious at having his private affairs discussed. So she left her sentence unfinished, and wondered privately and miserably how the loan was ever going to be paid, if even Whickery couldn't win.

Joan was still thinking about the oats. "I suppose all those horses do eat a lot," she said finally, and in a deflated tone.

"Yes, they do. And I eat a lot, not oats but other things, and so does Dad, and even Mother eats some." She smiled. "And the horses have to earn it all."

By the end of the week the news was more cheering. Whickery was entered in a second race, and Suzy was thrilled when Ben told her that Whickery had come in third.

"She's working up," he said. "When she comes home, she'll have a regular necklace of silver cups like those charm bracelets ladies wear. I know it in my bones. You be patient."

But being patient was the thing Suzy found hardest. At her next race, Whickery balked at the starting gate, got off to a late start, and came in the last of the field. The children at school were inclined to tease about this, for Suzy had boasted a good deal about Whickery, and the boys in particular kept asking to see Whickery's silver cups.

Joan was comforting, but it was not enough. Suzy wished spring vacation would *hurry up,* so she would not have to face her tormentors. But when it did come, she was sorry, for that was the week when Whickery got two firsts! There was a picture of her father standing at Whickery's head in the winner's circle, while he accepted the cup. Suzy cut out the picture, and planned to put it on the class bulletin board if her teacher would let her.

After the first few races in which she did so little, Whickery began to win almost monotonously. She was in the news, and the sports writers, who naturally had ignored her until she began to prove herself, now had something to say about her almost every day. In her first races, the purses Whickery won were not large, but as she went into the harder ones, against more experi-

enced horses, the purses increased in value. The important thing was that Whickery seemed to like to run. When she was led out to the track, her head lifted, she sniffed the air, and in general, as Ben said, "acted very prancy."

Mr. Taylor came home, and Suzy thought she had never seen him so gay. "If Whickery keeps this up — " he began a dozen times, "if Whickery keeps this up — "

"What, Dad, what?" Suzy was itching with curiosity and impatience.

"I'm afraid to say anything," said her father, laughing. "It might break the spell. But if she keeps on the way she's going, she'll get that loan paid off in a hurry. And filly or not, I'll enter her for the Derby."

"The Derby!" breathed Suzy, "the Derby!" Even she had aspired to that chiefly in her daydreams — in the excitement of the thought of the Derby she almost ignored what her father had said about clearing up the loan. But later, when she realized his meaning, little waves of relief and rapture flowed through her. Not to owe! "Why, we'd be, we'd be *free*," Suzy thought. "Our barn would really be our barn, and our farm *ours*." If the horses had an off year, it would be just an off year. Nothing would be threatened.

At this point in her thoughts, Suzy went out and took a look at the training barn which had been the source of so many of her worries. Miraculously, it was no longer a "black" barn; with the loan paid off, its menace was gone. Now it looked like just what it was, a comfortable

place for horses in training to stay. A load Suzy hadn't realized she was carrying slid quietly off her shoulders. She felt curiously light and very happy. "Whickery's the one doing it," she thought, "but I've helped. Dad and Ben both say so — "

"Suzy — " That was Ben's voice calling. Here she was, standing around thinking how good she was, and leaving poor Ben to do all the chores. She grabbed a bucket and ran off to help.

When Whickery returned home at the end of the racing season, she did not wear a necklace of trophies as Ben had predicted, but she did bring a dozen.

"Twelve wins out of eighteen starts," Mr. Taylor said. "It's phenomenal. I still don't quite believe it."

"I knew she was special from the minute she was born!" Suzy sounded smug. "Whickering like that when she was barely in the world. She'd just have to be special."

Most of the horses who had been off at different tracks, had now come home and had been turned out to rest and relax for a while. They would be "picked up" again, as the trainer called it, in time to get into condition before the autumn season began.

"We'll see how Whickery does this fall," Mr. Taylor said in answer to Suzy's many questions, "and if she's still winning like crazy, we'll get bigger and better ideas." And this was as far as he would go.

Suzy herself thought of little but the Derby. She kept

a scrapbook of Whickery's races through the autumn, and as the book slowly fattened and the number of victories grew, she wondered how her father could hesitate.

But he said, "It's a mile and a quarter race. Whickery has done marvelously up to a mile and an eighth. Now an eighth's two hundred and twenty yards. That gives a horse with staying power plenty of time to come up from behind and get there first. We've got to find out if Whickery has the stamina for that last eighth of a mile. It costs sixteen hundred dollars to race her in the Derby. I'm thinking about it."

It was the chief thought of everyone on the farm. Suzy noticed that Whickery was being put in longer races, and when she was training at home, she was usually breezed for a mile and a half.

"To give her some margin," Mr. Taylor said.

At last the time came when the decision had to be made. Suzy followed her father around like a too persistent puppy until he finally threatened to shut her up in an empty stall. She was insulted and avoided him the rest of the day, but her hurt feelings were forgotten when her father said at the supper table, "I clocked Whickery at two minutes, three seconds, for a mile and a quarter this morning. That's within five seconds of the world's record."

Suzy looked at him, unable for a moment to speak. "Then you're going to — "

"I'm entering her. The check goes off tonight."

Suzy was so excited she could hardly eat her supper, and the minute it was over, she rushed to the telephone to tell Joan.

"Can you go to the Derby?" Joan asked, and Suzy couldn't answer because suddenly there was a huge lump in her throat that took her voice away.

She said nothing to her parents about her feeling of heartbreak at not going to the Derby. After all, no one could argue with what Daddy had said about being honest and playing the game by the rules. And there the rules were, rising like a high fence between her and the race track. If there were only a knothole in that fence!

In the meantime, even if she couldn't go to the race, Suzy shared in all the excitement of preparation. The big van was out again and the partitions at one end removed so that in effect Whickery had a big box stall. A stall was kept at the other end for the lead pony, for Whickery would be nervous if she had to go off without her friends.

Joan was sitting on the fence with Suzy, watching the preparations. "You can't go, but I suppose that goat can," she said. Joan disliked Billy, who loved to steal up behind her and butt her with his horns.

Suzy thought she would be the happiest girl in the world if she could ride down to Kentucky in the van with Whickery, but there was no use dreaming any longer of that. She said, almost crossly, "You know I can't go. And Whickery needs Billy — not me."

At that moment Whickery was led across the yard to

the van. Suzy thought she never had looked so beautiful. Her bay coat was brilliantly glossy, and the white star on her forehead and her three white socks looked freshly scrubbed. The girls hopped off the fence and ran over to tell her good-by. Suzy put her arms around the proud, arching neck and began to rub her gently. Whickery bent her head to feel around for her carrot and pulled two out of Suzy's pockets. She munched a minute and then sniffed Joan, who handed over her own apple.

"Stop sweet-talking that filly," Ben said. "We got to get loaded and be on our way."

The girls reluctantly stepped back, but not until Suzy had given Whickery a warm kiss on her soft velvet nose. Whickery was used to the van by now and walked up the ramp as nonchalantly as if she had always thought it nothing. Once in the truck she turned and, poking her head out the door, gave a long whicker.

"That's horse language for saying she's going to win the Derby," said Suzy. Joan laughed, but they both felt sure it was true. They watched until the van rounded the curve, and once again they heard the same long whicker.

"What's she saying this time?" Joan asked, grinning.

"She says she's really going to win, she's not fooling."

The van was out of sight, but Suzy still stood staring after it. It would be glorious, *glorious* to have a Derby winner! And a winner bred, born, and trained on their own farm!

"What's the matter?" Joan asked, looking at Suzy's

tranced face and giving her a poke. "You look like Christmas morning."

Suzy shook herself and laughed. "Listen!" she said, and held up a finger. A faint nicker came to them from the van now far down the road.

"That's still Whickery," said Suzy, " for the last time, telling me not to worry. She says she's going to eat her oats yet out of that Derby cup."

The Derby was still more than two weeks away. Whickery had been sent off early in order to have time to rest up from the trip, and to get used to conditions at the Kentucky track. Suzy rarely mentioned the race now, but was inclined to mope as she watched her parents' preparations to go. Her pale looks and silent unhappiness had not gone unnoticed by her parents.

"I'm awfully sorry, old girl," her father began one day, but Suzy interrupted with a strangled, "Don't talk about it!" and she rushed off to Whickery's stall to weep in private.

Later, she saw her father and mother reading a letter jointly. "It's very persuasive," her mother said.

"If this doesn't do it, nothing would," said Mr. Taylor modestly. Turning to his daughter, he asked, "Have you got a dollar?"

"Yes, sir." Suzy ran up to her room to fetch it, wondering what in the world Daddy wanted with *her* dollar. She gave him the money, and he made her a bow and, handing her an official-looking paper with a notary's seal, said, "Read this."

Suzy read, at first not quite understanding the legal terms. But there it was: "for the sum of $1 and other good and lawful considerations" — she — why, she was part owner of Whickery!

"Daddy," she began, "Daddy — " and could say no more.

"Don't smile any wider," said her mother, laughing. "Your cheeks will split."

Suzy laughed, too, but before she could say anything, her father said, "You've earned this. You worked hard, and your help was important. And as part owner, maybe you'll get some privileges — " but at this point he broke off.

"I want that paper," said Suzy. "I'll have it framed and hang it in my room."

"I need it to enclose in my letter. But it will be returned to me and then I'll give it to you." He slipped the affidavit in the waiting envelope.

Suzy felt she had to share her joy and excitement, so she ran out to the stable and saddled Elsinore. Joan lived just a mile away, and it was an easy canter over through the fields.

The race was now only a few days off, and suitcases were brought out to be packed, for naturally both Mr. and Mrs. Taylor were going. Suzy tried not to feel envious, but she could not help looking at them with longing eyes.

If only she could go, too! Her parents tried to console her. "In another two or three years," her mother began, but Suzy said stonily, "Oh, Mother, stop. *This* is the race

I want to see. We may never have another horse good enough to be in the Derby. I heard a trainer talking to ours, and he said they'd been breeding for twenty years and hadn't yet come up with a Derby horse. Isn't that often true, Dad?" she asked, turning to her father.

"It is," he answered slowly. "Horses — and people — may have equally good heredity, but along comes one horse — or one man who happens to be a genius — or a Derby winner. It's like lightning striking. You know it will strike, but you never know just when or how or where."

"Don't forget the Derby will be on television," Mrs. Taylor persisted. "That's better than just reading about it. And I'll notice — and remember — every detail, and tell you *everything* when we get home."

Suzy swallowed. "Thank you, Mother," she said in a low voice, and left the room. She wasn't going to let one tear squeeze out. She thought if she went to Whickery's empty stall she'd feel closer to her and better for it. After a while, she did feel better, and went back determined to be as cheerful as she could.

The next morning at breakfast the talk was naturally all of the trip. Ben brought the mail in, and Mr. Taylor ran through it hurriedly until he found a long envelope. "This is it," he said to his wife. "I'm a little afraid to open it."

"Give it to me then," said Mrs. Taylor, but he had already slit the envelope. He unfolded and read the letter quickly, read it again with a grin, and handed it to his wife. In addition to the letter, there were two enclosures, which he opened carefully. One was the affidavit he had sent, and the other a square of parchment, magnificent with blue ribbon and red sealing wax. Mr. Taylor looked at it and whistled, then held it up for Mrs. Taylor and Suzy to see.

"What *is* it, Jim?" asked Mrs. Taylor.

Smiling at Suzy, her father turned the official-looking document around and read the important part aloud: "Know ye, that reposing special trust and confidence in the patriotism, valor, fidelity, and abilities of Susan Taylor, I do hereby appoint her an honorary commissioned officer, in the grade of colonel."

He handed the parchment to Suzy. "This means you are an honorary colonel on the staff of the Governor of Kentucky. You'll get to the race, all right, with this!"

"Me a *colonel!*" Suzy gasped. "How, Daddy?" Her eyes got so big that her mother said nervously, "Suzy! Suzy! Come back to earth. You look ready to float away."

Mr. Taylor, looking unbearably smug, said, "Virtue is being rewarded. At the same time that I sent the affidavit to the Racing Commission, and asked for permission for you as joint owner to be admitted to the tracks, I wrote to one of my Kentucky breeder friends, Harry Banton. I asked him to write the Commission, too, and tell them this was all in good faith, that you had worked hard and were legally part owner of Whickery. He did better than that. Part owner or not, it seems they wouldn't let you in. So he called the Governor, who is a friend of his, and asked what he would suggest. The

Governor thought of the honorary commission and is-
sued it. They issue some each year — you know how
everybody talks about Kentucky colonels. I suppose the
Governor thought it would make a good human-interest
story reflecting credit on him. It does, too. Maybe that's
not the way it was, but that's my guess."

"Me a colonel!" Suzy repeated, her voice still breathless. "Is it really true, Dad? Do you suppose I'll have a
uniform?"

"No uniform. You're an *honorary* colonel. But you'll
get to the race."

"You ought to have a new dress, though," said her
mother. "Not sophisticated, but more so than your
usual things. Maybe we could drive in to Richmond this
afternoon and see what we could find."

Suzy, absorbed in rapturous thoughts, made no reply.
A moment later the school bus blew twice impatiently,
but she still heard nothing.

Mrs. Taylor looked at her husband. "She'll just have
to be late this morning. Give her time to calm down.
We all need to. I'll drive her over later."

He nodded and started for the stables.

Chapter ELEVEN

SUZY AND HER PARENTS made the long drive to Kentucky and arrived the day before the race. They drove out to the track at once, as Whickery was stabled nearby. At Suzy's insistence, they paused only to buy some apples and carrots for Whickery.

As they got out of the car, the trainer walked over to meet them, Jo-Boy rushed up, and Billy sailed over the paddock fence and landed near them. He gave Suzy a playful butt, but she had eyes only for Whickery who stood watching their arrival, her head over the small paddock fence.

"In fine shape," the trainer was saying. "Couldn't ask for better." But Suzy heard nothing. She rushed to the paddock fence, was over it almost as quickly as Billy had come the other way, and now stood with one arm around Whickery's neck, gently scratching her. In her other hand was the carrot which Whickery instantly took. After munching it, she began running her lips over Suzy, hunting for pockets in which more carrots might be concealed.

Suzy crowed. "She knows I'm part owner. She's kissing me all over!"

"She's not kissing — she's hunting for carrots, as you very well know. Give her another," said her father, handing her the bag.

That night at the hotel, Suzy was sure she could never go to sleep. Her father and mother had gone out to a Breeders' Association dinner, and Suzy was alone. Her own dinner was served upstairs. After eating it, she wandered restlessly around her room. There was nothing to do except to think worriedly about tomorrow's race. After a while, remembering her promise to her mother, she undressed reluctantly and got into bed. "I wonder what it will be like to stay awake all night," she thought, and it was her last thought until the next morning.

The sun was streaming into her room, across the bed, into her eyes, and there was her mother — standing at the foot of the bed and smiling at her. "Nine o'clock," said Mrs. Taylor. "You must have been exhausted."

"I'm not now, though!" Suzy bounced up in bed, running her fingers through her red curls. "Where's Dad?"

"He's gone out to the track. He has business to attend to and he didn't want the women along. But we're to meet him for an early lunch, and we'll see Whickery before the race."

146

In a way Suzy was glad she had slept late as it made the morning shorter. She and her mother dressed carefully, and with the colonel's badge pinned on her dress and her commission in her hand, she was ready to go. When her father came in to get them, he looked Suzy over and said, "Better put that commission away. You won't need it."

"I'd feel safer, just in case — "

"In my vest pocket, then. You'll lose it sure if you carry it in your hand."

Time edged along slowly, though there were periods when Suzy thought it had stopped entirely. Eventually, they were at the track.

"Don't forget to thank Mr. Banton for getting you the commission," her father reminded her.

As if she could! Suzy sometimes thought grown people must all be crazy. Mr. Banton met them at the gate and escorted them in, "on the chance that anyone questions your being here," he said, smiling. One of the guards did start toward them, but with Mr. Banton to explain, she was soon safely past him, past the gateman, and in the grandstand, seated in Mr. Banton's box with her parents.

The grandstand was full, people milling about, calling to friends, laughing, talking, excited. Suzy looked at the crowd around her. Inside the fence separating them from the track were the standees, thousands of them, packed in but still able to move a bit, a riot of moving color gay as a kaleidoscope. A few people — they must have come at daybreak, Suzy thought — were perched on canes with hunting seats near the fence.

"Take my glasses, Sue," said her father, "and look across the track."

She adjusted the field glasses and stared. On the far side of the fence and outside it were a few people. They had brought tall stepladders and were standing on them, looking around.

"If they had just brought a plain ladder," said her father, "and leaned it against the fence, the authorities would clear them out in no time. But technically they're not trespassing, so I guess they'll stay where they are."

"Oh-h-h!" said Suzy, still peering through the glasses. A stepladder had collapsed, and the three men who had been standing on it had disappeared.

"Don't worry. They'll bounce back."

Suzy could hardly believe that, and expected to see an ambulance, stretchers, broken arms and legs, but in a moment the ladder reappeared, and the same men were climbing it again. Two were rubbing sore spots gingerly, but the other one seemed as unconcerned as if he had just gone out for a smoke.

The sun shone brilliantly, flags flew in the gentle breeze, the mass of people rustled, talked, an occasional whinny came from the direction of the stables, and Suzy thought she had never seen anything so gay, so nearly *perfect*.

She had not realized there would be preliminary races before the Derby itself, but finally they were over, and she and her parents, together with other owners, went down to see the entries for the big race saddled up. The trainer was there with a stable boy, and he greeted them with a nervous smile. "Whickery feels fine," he said. "I'm the one with the jitters."

Just then a bell clanged. "There goes the 'saddle up,'" the trainer observed, and in a moment the small English saddle with what seemed to Suzy ridiculously short stirrups was over Whickery's back. Meanwhile the trainer and a track official were running their hands up and down Whickery's legs, looking in her mouth and up her nose, and generally checking her over carefully.

"They do this to all the horses," Mr. Taylor told Suzy, noticing her suspicious looks. "They want to be sure the horses haven't been tampered with. This way there's no chance of any unwarranted claims of fouls."

The bell clanged a second time, the trainer checked the bridle and girth strap, and a stable boy ran to Whickery's head and started leading her around the small walking ring. She had a big 4 on her blanket, and Suzy stared at it angrily.

"What do they mean, she's Number 4?"

"That's the number she drew," the trainer told her, "and it's put on so the people betting on her can identify her. It means, too, she gets the number 4 slot in the starting gate." He turned away to greet the jockey who came up, dressed in the blue and white silks that were the official farm colors.

"He's tiny," Suzy thought. "Why, I'm as tall as he is! And I'll bet I weigh more."

Mac was speaking to her father. "I've got two pounds of lead in my saddle pockets, Mr. Taylor. I did such a good job of reducing, I've got to carry the lead to make the weight."

Just then the bell rang for the third time. "That's the bell that says, 'Put your riders up,'" Mr. Taylor explained.

In another moment, with a flashing of colors from all the jockeys' brilliant silks, the horses were mounted and led out to the track. As they appeared, the bugles sounded, and Suzy thought again she had never seen anything so gay, as the crowds stirred in excitement and chatter. The stable boys leading the horses now released them, and the jockeys began to warm up their mounts by first walking, then trotting, then cantering a short distance down the track.

The three Taylors made their way back to the box, Suzy still full of questions. "Why does Mac have to carry that lead in his saddle pockets?" she asked.

"Because every horse is supposed to have an equal chance. Each extra two pounds a horse carries costs him a length in distance. Don't ask any more questions now. The horses are going to the gate."

Mr. Taylor picked up his field glasses and looked

across the track. "Whickery seems as calm as if she were on the track at home," he said, handing the glasses to his wife. She passed them quickly to Suzy, who looked anxiously to see if Whickery were acting up about the gate. Mac was patting her, and Suzy thought it must be with real affection. Whickery seemed almost nonchalant.

"Listen carefully, Sue," said her father. "The race will be starting in about two minutes. There are eleven other owners here with as high hopes as we have. Win or lose, behave yourself. Don't crow if we win, don't cry if we don't. You're with a bunch of sportsmen, so act like one."

"I will. You didn't need to say it."

"No, you didn't, Jim," said Mrs. Taylor.

"People get excited. She's the youngest person here." He picked up his glasses again. "Seems to be a little trouble at the gate. Number 2 is trying to climb over it."

Number 2 came down on his four feet again. A second later, the whistle blew, and the announcer's voice called — "They're off!"

Suzy strained to see what was going on, but their box was near the finish line, and the horses were on the opposite side of the track. The announcer kept up a rapid fire of information but Suzy heard only what he said about Whickery. At the quarter post, Whickery was sixth in the field, then she fell back to seventh, then eighth. Suzy thought her heart would stop beating. Her father had his glasses up, following intently; a glance at him showed he was not upset. Eighth place! — how could he take it so calmly?

Suddenly an opening appeared in the crowded group of horses. Mac shot Whickery through it — and there she was, next the rail, the best position of all.

"Whickery's coming up," the announcer boomed. "She's in sixth place — no, fifth. Now they're entering the stretch!"

As at a signal the crowd rose to its feet. Voices were heard shouting, "Come on, Gunner! Come on, Silver Prince!"

"Come on, Whickery!" Suzy shouted.

Her father patted her shoulder. "She will. She will. A horse can only run its very fastest for twenty seconds; she's been saving up for this."

The jumble of horses began to lengthen out as they tore down the stretch. Silver Prince had led but was now back in fourth place. Gunner was fighting to keep the lead but Whickery was pressing close behind him.

"The favorite's falling back!" the announcer shouted. "Whickery's worked up from eighth place to third, and she's still gaining. Silver Prince — " but Suzy heard nothing of Silver Prince. There — before her eyes — Whickery was gaining — gaining — ! Mac was lashing her with his whip. He ought not to, he ought not to — But at that instant Whickery seemed to leap ahead, her stride unbelievably long. She was even with Silver Prince, she was past him — she was across the finish line, ahead by a neck!

The crowd was jumping up and down and shouting, but Suzy felt weak. Whickery was the winner. She had done it! Suzy had been sure she would — and yet . . . and yet . . . she'd been so afraid she wouldn't. But it had happened! Her father turned and gave her a great hug. "She did it!" he said. "Our horse! We knew it all the time, didn't we, but now we *really* know!"

The horses had been going too fast to stop at the finish line, and continued on down the track for a quarter of a mile. But their speed had decreased, the jockeys rated them down, and some were already turning around and walking their mounts back to the finish line. As they reached this point, the stable boys came forward to claim their horses; the jockeys dismounted and started for the stables with their saddles over their arms.

In the meantime, officials had come up to Mr. Taylor. "Come on, Sue," he said. "We are going down to the winner's circle." She hurried after her father and mother, down the grandstand steps, and out to the circle. Whickery was waiting there, Mac at her head, powdered with dust and dirt, but with a wide grin on his face.

"We did it, Mr. Taylor," he said exultantly. "When we were so far back, I got a little nervous, but Whickery never was."

"Quiet now," said one of the officials, "the Governor is going to present the trophy."

Her father and mother stood very straight while the

Governor talked and the cameras clicked. Suzy heard hardly a word he said. There was Whickery, she wanted to go over and pet her, but her father held her arm tightly and anchored her to his side.

"And so," the Governor was obviously concluding, "it gives me great pleasure to present this trophy to Mr. James Taylor of Cherrydale Farm, and to a member of my own staff, Miss Susan Taylor, co-owner of the winner."

There was such a buzzing in her ears that Suzy thought a flight of airplanes must be passing overhead. But it was only joy, she realized in surprise. Prodded by her father, she stepped forward with him to receive the trophy. "Give it to your mother," he whispered, and as she did so the applauding crowd began to whistle and stamp.

"Now lead Whickery up," her father said, and Suzy gladly took the lead rein from the stable boy. Whickery immediately began to nuzzle her and look for carrots, and seemed rather more annoyed than pleased when the Governor slipped the winner's garland over her neck.

"I have a carrot for her, Daddy," said Suzy, fumbling in her handbag.

"Careful what you say there," he said, laughing. "We're on television, you know."

Television! That would be something sure enough to tell Joan. But of course she was watching!

"Now a few words from you, Mr. Taylor," the camera

man was saying, and a minute later he turned to Suzy. "We'd like to hear from the co-owner, Colonel Susan Taylor."

Suzy stared at the unfamiliar microphone and then seized it. "Whickery was bred, born, and trained on our farm. She was special from the minute she was born. I always knew she could win even a wonderful race like the Derby. And she has."

She put her arms around Whickery's neck and kissed her on her soft, trembling nose.